Speak to Me in Indian

DAVID GIDMARK

Speak to Me in Indian

A Novel

Baraka Books

Montréal

ISBN 978-1-77186-053-6 pbk; 978-177186-055-0 epub; 978-177186-056-7 pdf; 978-177186-057-4 mobi/kindle

Front cover photo by David Gidmark
Back cover photo by Julia Philpot

Cover by Folio infographie
Book design by Folio infographie
Legal Deposit, 3rd quarter 2015

Bibliothèque et Archives nationales du Québec
Library and Archives Canada
Published by Baraka Books of Montreal.
6977, rue Lacroix
Montréal, Québec H4E 2V4
Telephone: 514 808-8504
info@barakabooks.com
www.barakabooks.com

Printed and bound in Quebec

We acknowledge the support from the Société de développement des entreprises culturelles (SODEC) and the Government of Quebec tax credit for book publishing administered by SODEC.

Société
de développement
des entreprises
culturelles
Québec

We acknowledge the support of the Canada Council for the Arts, which last year invested $153 million to bring the arts to Canadians throughout the country.

Financé par le gouvernement du Canada
Funded by the Government of Canada | Canada

Trade Distribution & Returns
Canada and the United States
Independent Publishers Group
1-800-888-4741 (IPG1);
orders@ipgbook.com

To Ernestine

Chapter One

"Why doesn't he talk to us?"

"He speaks only Indian."

The three Indian guides were readying canvas canoes for a day's speckled-trout fishing. The sun was mounting the eastern slopes of the hills surrounding Lac du Rocher. Mist was upon the mirror-like surface of the wilderness lake. The lake was one of Earth's eyes. The three guides and the three white fishermen had spent the night in the small lodge on Lac du Rocher. They had flown in the day before from an outfitter's camp on Lac Brascoupé.

One of the tourists, a large man, sat in the bow seat of Basil Carle's canoe. Basil weighed one hundred pounds, and the white tourist well over two hundred; the trim was terribly off.

"You can't go like that," said Jocko Whiteduck, Basil's trapping partner and the foreman of the guides at Lac Brascoupé. Basil looked at the bow of his canoe, much too low in the water under the weight of the white fisherman, and he laughed.

Jocko motioned to one of the other fisherman, a man who weighed around a hundred and sixty pounds, to change places with the man in Basil's bow. "That's better," Jocko said, "It's still not too good though." He went to his own canoe, took out the heavy, wooden grub-box with the tumpline attached and placed it just fore of Basil in the canoe.

The man in Basil's canoe looked back, hoping that the canoe would soon be sitting level in the water, and that they could depart. "It's not the best even now," Jocko said, looking at the awkward trim. Turning to the man in the bow, he said, "Take the change out of your pockets."

The man had both hands in his pockets before he realized he was being teased.

II

Two white-throated sparrows and one wood duck called to their brethren that there were human visitors on the lake. The three canoes glided south across Lac du Rocher towards the portage. The guides in the stern paddled smoothly; the tourists much less so. In early August, a mist over the lake meant that the night had been cold but the day would be warm.

Jocko Whiteduck and Basil Carle were Algonquins in their seventies from the Algonquin reservation in Maniwaki. Jocko was a strong, stocky man; age had brought a stoop into his walk. The fact that his family name came from the white duck (*wabicib*) and that he now had short-cropped white hair could be credited only to coincidence and age.

Basil Carle was strong but extremely thin; the hair that came to his shoulders was gray, but not entirely so. His walk suggested — quite falsely — the feebleness of an old man. He was hard of hearing, but there was no one among the twenty guides at Lac Brascoupé more renowned for good humour and graciousness.

The third guide, Angus Wawati, was a very powerful man in his early fifties. He was an Algonquin from Ottawa Lake, far to the northeast. He had dark, tawny skin and long hair, still jet black. His faced was unlined. Where Jocko and Basil showed a small admixture of white blood, Angus showed none.

Angus looked older than his two Indian friends — not in years, but in epochs. Angus seemed as though he was from the sixteenth century.

Ted, the man in Jocko's bow, was tall, thin, quiet, and he paid close attention to everything the guides did. He'd been coming to Lac Brascoupé for decades. The other two fishermen — the big man in Angus's canoe and the smaller one in Basil's — were neophytes.

The tourist in Basil's bow talked a lot, which was one reason Jocko put the man with Basil.

"Basil's hard of hearing?" the man asked.

Jocko said from his canoe, twenty feet away, "He's been like that since the 1930s."

"What happened?"

"He was working on the Gatineau River for the lumber company. He was with his two brothers in a boat trying to get a logjam free. They were using dynamite and it blew up. One of the brothers was killed; the other is alright. Basil's hearing went bad."

"I know he speaks English well," the tourist said. "I don't have any trouble understanding him when he speaks, but I've got to do some ungodly shouting for him to hear me."

"Anin gai ikitotc?" Basil asked, wanting to know what the man was saying. Jocko told him that the man was inquiring about his hearing problem. Basil just laughed.

"I'd swear that Basil *hears* better when you speak in Indian," the man said to Jocko. Jocko didn't say anything.

Ted was paddling in the bow of Jocko's canoe, paddling nearly as skilfully as the three guides, and with a minimum of talk. Now he spoke: "Basil has a gentlemanliness, good humour, gentleness, and considerateness that we'll never match. Maybe it's in their genes."

The talkative tourist: "I don't understand."

Ted: "No, you don't understand."

They paddled in silence for a while. The talkative tourist could not keep quiet for long though. "And Angus doesn't speak anything but Indian?" he asked.

Jocko by this time was hoping that they could just keep paddling without the noise. "That's a real Indian," Jocko said, in answer to the question, more or less, and referring to Angus. Then to Angus he said, speaking in Indian, "Maybe we should get a radio."

Angus didn't say anything, but only continued his smooth paddling.

Jocko liked Ted, the white fisherman in the bow of his canoe. Ted had been coming to Brascoupé for more than thirty years, first as a teenager with his parents. He'd been keen about learning; he was acquiring a knowledge of the woods. And the more time he spent at Brascoupé the quieter he became, something that Jocko appreciated.

The friend in Basil's canoe was making his first visit to the area. The fact seemed to be reflected in the man's loquaciousness.

"Ted, where'd you learn to paddle like that?" the talkative man asked

"From them," Ted said, indicating Jocko and Basil.

"Do Indians know everything about the woods?" Basil's canoe mate asked.

Angus did not respond because he couldn't understand; Basil because he couldn't hear; Jocko because he did not think the comment worthy of response.

The tourist rephrased the question. "Indians seem to know a lot about the woods."

Jocko, effacing himself and Basil in deference to Angus, nodded in the direction of Angus Wawati and said, "He does."

Basil asked Angus and Jocko, in Indian, if they'd stop paddling a moment. He lit his pipe; then they continued.

Off to the left of the canoes, a loon wailed. "She's looking for her baby," Jocko said.

The sunlight was beginning to absorb the mist. Several white-throated sparrows in the woods on the shore gave distinctive whistles; they seemed enthusiastic about having visitors.

A gray owl flew over the canoes. "He's going to start his day's hunting," Jocko said.

They arrived at the portage. As they brought the canoes up on shore, the fisherman in Basil's canoe said, "How do we do this?" He made ready to pick up the canoe on one end to help Basil carry the canoe over the portage.

"It's best just to stay out of the way," Basil said politely.

"But you can't carry that by yourself," the fisherman asserted. He shouted the same thing to Basil three times, but Basil couldn't or wouldn't hear. He looked at Jocko. "Basil's in his seventies, and he hardly weighs 100 pounds. How the hell is he going to carry that?"

Jocko said only, "It's best to stay out of the way."

Basil carefully shouldered the canoe and was off down the portage trail to the next lake. Angus and Jocko shouldered their canoes; Ted carried the heavy, wooden grub box with the tumpline, and the other two carried the fishing poles and the tackle boxes.

At the end of the short portage, they came into Lac à la Bague. The three guides carrying the canoes and the three fishermen were winded, about equally. But the talkative one said, "Damn, you know, back at Brascoupé I was walking alongside Basil and Jocko from the cookhouse to the dock this morning. I had to slow down so they could catch up, and I said to myself they're old men in their seventies. But I'd swear they walk faster than we do in the woods."

They put their gear in the canoes and started paddling through the marshy margin of the lake.

"*Acagi*," Angus was heard to say.

"What did he say?" one of the fishermen asked.

Jocko thought a minute to find the English translation. "That's a blue heron."

"I don't see any blue heron," the tourist said, looking around on both sides of the canoe through the marsh. Jocko, Angus, and Basil kept paddling smoothly through the water.

Then, when the fisherman had given up looking, a harsh croak on the starboard side of the canoes startled him. In contrast to the harsh croaks, the flight of the heron as it lifted from the lake was full of grace. They watched the large bird disappear over the trees at the end of the lake.

They paddled on through the small lake — this one, like the larger Lac du Rocher, perfectly smooth in the early morning. The elegant canoes cut the aqueous mirror sharply but quietly and left in their wakes exquisitely sculpted little ripples.

It was Basil's tourist who betrayed the silence. "Maybe if we fished in this lake, we wouldn't have to make the long portage to the next one."

Basil couldn't hear; Angus couldn't understand; and Jocko hoped that if he remained silent, the man's thought would pass.

They reached the portage at the end of Lac à la Bague. The canoes and gear were on shore. Ted again picked up the heavy, wooden grub box and was about to put the tumpline around his forehead.

The fisherman who had been in Angus's bow came up to him. "Ted," he said, "let me try that gismo." He indicated the grub box with the tumpline attached.

"It's heavy," Ted said.

"No offense, Ted, but I'm bigger than you are."

Ted helped him put the grub box on the small of his back while he tried to fix the tumpline comfortably on the man's forehead. "Oh, God!" the man exclaimed as the full weight of the box drew back on his neck.

"You want me to take it?" Ted asked.

"No, I'll make it," the stout fisherman said as he started off down the trail, staggering every few steps. The three guides followed with the canoes. Ted and the other fisherman carried the fishing gear.

The portage was half-a-mile long. Angus, canoe on his shoulders, followed the man with the grub box. The man stumbled and nearly fell. The trail rose. There was no way Angus could pass him on the narrow trail. The man tired. Finally, he stumbled and fell.

Angus saw his chance. He walked up to the man and carefully put the canoe on the ground. His powerful arms picked up the grub box by the tumpline straps. He carefully fixed the tumpline on his forehead. Then he backed over to the canoe. Balancing the grub box on his back, he bent down to grab the canoe by the gunwales. As he lifted one side of the canoe up, he quickly put an arm around the bottom of the canoe, lifted it to chest height, and onto his shoulders. Then he walked up the trail with both the grub box and the canoe.

The party had to go through a short, rocky channel at the small lake at the end of the portage. Jocko and Angus and their canoes negotiated the rapids first. Basil followed in his canoe with the talkative tourist.

As they were passing the last rock, the fisherman shoved at the rock with his paddle. The paddle became wedged between two rocks, and the speed of the canoe caused it to break. Only quick correction by Basil kept the canoe from capsizing. Jocko, watching from below, gave a barely perceptible grimace that indicated impatience. Having only one paddle in a canoe would slow them all down.

The fisherman, having broken his paddle, seemed to feel that not having to paddle freed up more time for him to talk. "Are we going to catch any speckled trout today?" he asked.

Jocko, somewhat impatiently, said, "Oh, I think so."

"How can we be sure?"

"Because you've got three good Indian guides," Jocko said.

"*Monz,*" Angus said.

"What did he say?"

"There's a moose around," Jocko said. Then he looked to the far end of the lake, half-a-mile off, squinted a few moments and finally located the moose browsing on the grasses in the lake. He paddled close to the other canoes. "Stop paddling," he told the three fishermen. "Don't make any noise." Then to

Angus: "*Kit ijamin indi.*" And the three Indians paddled the canoes quietly in the direction of the moose.

One hundred yards from the moose, the three guides switched to a silent paddle stroke that kept the paddles underwater. They approached the moose within thirty feet until someone in one of the canoes moved his foot.

The moose, still slowly chewing the weeds, looked up in the direction of the canoes. It turned and, in what seemed to be slow motion, ambled off into the woods.

III

At the end of the lake, the three fishermen busied themselves baiting their lines. Ted used worms; the other two used spinners. Basil smoked a pipe; Jocko exchanged a few words with Angus.

The little lake where they fished was hidden from other fishermen. Were it not for that, catching speckled trout in early August would have been difficult.

The three men soon caught six large, speckled trout, one for each of the party. Basil's tourist wanted to continue fishing.

"That's enough," Jocko said.

"I'm going to fix a shore lunch," Basil said.

They pulled their canoes onto a low, flat granite rock that appeared to lie upon the surface of the water at the edge of the lake.

"Can I help you with the lunch, Basil?" Ted asked.

"Eh?" Basil said.

When Ted repeated the question in a louder voice, Basil replied, "Why sure!"

Ted cleaned the fish; the two other fishermen gathered dry wood for the fire. Basil took out two large frying pans and a small one from the grub box. Jocko removed the flour, butter, bacon grease, and camp beans from the box.

Angus did a strange thing. He walked back in the woods about twenty feet from the camp and looked closely at a birch tree that was eight inches in diameter. He walked around it, assessing it carefully. He checked the sharpness of his medium-sized axe by pulling up his shirt sleeve and shaving a few hairs on his arm. Then he started to chop the tree at the base. When the tree was down, he chopped a five-foot log, working slowly but well.

Basil's tourist had been busy gathering dry wood with the other fisherman. Bringing an armload back to the fire, he looked over at Angus for the first time. He was surprised, then incredulous. Jocko saw the tourist looking at Angus working on the birch log, and Jocko could read the man's look quite well. The look said: "My God, doesn't this poor fellow know that you make a fire with dry wood, not green wood?" Jocko did not feel that the incredulous look needed a response.

Hitting the axe head with a small block of wood, Angus split his birch log into halves and then quarters. Then he put one of the quarters on a stump and began shaping it with his sharp axe. After taking off much of the wood, he sat on the stump and took out his crooked knife, a curved knife that he pulled toward him in quick, smooth, deft strokes.

Basil laid several even, straight dry-spruce sticks over the fire to form a burning grate. Ted had dipped the trout fillets in flour and was putting some bacon grease in the frying pan. "Put a little butter in the bacon grease too," Basil told Ted. "Not too much."

"I'm getting hungry already," Jocko said. "Good thing you people know how to catch fish." Despite his occasional scepticism, Jocko liked being with these white men — and he liked being in the woods.

Basil had readied the potatoes and onions. Jocko took out the beans that had been baking overnight back at the cookhouse on Lac Brascoupé. He held the bean pot out to one of the tourists. "We call them camp beans," he said, fanning the flames of his own enthusiasm for the meal even more.

"Boil the tea," Basil said to Ted. Ted found a long forked stick that he then propped at an angle over the fire with two large rocks. Then he took a large aluminum can with a wire attached to it, filled it from the lake, and hung it at the end of the stick over the fire. The other two tourists busied themselves taking out the plates and the knives and forks.

The midday sun was warm now. The leaves of some of the poplars fluttered in the light breeze. The pristine fragrance of the balsam mingled with the rich smell of the trout frying in bacon grease. Two gulls flew over to spy upon the source of the excitement. Some of the men, seduced by the aroma, became restless in their hunger. The meal was ready an hour after the party had landed on the rock.

Basil dished up a plate and handed it to the man who had been in his bow. Just as the man took the plate, there was a tap on his shoulder. The fellow looked around in surprise.

It was Angus, with a sly smile on his face. "*Manadj kâpina-man âbwi nongom*," he said, handing him a beautifully crafted birch paddle.

"What did he say?" he asked Jocko.

"He says, 'Be careful with the paddle this time,'" Jocko said.

They all ate with great satisfaction and to repletion. Someone remarked that it was lucky that the trout were so large. They sat quietly after they finished. The water in the tea pail, suspended from the cooking stick, was now boiling. Ted asked Jocko if he should put some tea in the water. This caused one of the other men to ask, "Didn't Indians get tea from the woods years ago?"

"Anin gai ikitotc?" Angus asked Jocko. Jocko translated for him.

Angus put his fork on his plate, and then set the plate down. He turned to his right and with both hands plucked the leaves of the Labrador tea plant. He rose and put them in the boiling water before Ted could find the tea in the grub box.

They drank their tea in silence. Some of the men had already mentioned the wild profusion of blueberries. Now it was Ted who said, "If we only had a good blueberry pie."

"Anin gai ikitotc?" Angus said to Jocko.

"Wi midjin minan tebate, gai ikito," he told Angus.

Angus thought a moment. He said to Jocko, *"Apic ot ickva minikwewatc, ta minikek."*

Now it was Ted's turn to ask, "What did he say?"

"He says that when you finish your tea, you should all go pick some blueberries."

In a few minutes, the three men walked off to the blueberries, one using the clean bean pot as a container, the other two employing two large hats.

"Ki ta andawabandan wîkwâs," Angus said to Basil, and the latter dutifully walked off to the downed birch log to cut out a clean sheet of birch-bark.

Angus mixed flour and lard. Basil returned with the sheet of birch-bark. He laid it down on the ground in front of Angus, the clean, tawny interior surface facing up.

Angus had two big balls of dough, but then he stopped. "*Obotei ni manesin*," he said to Jocko. Jocko called to one of the tourists in the blueberry patch, "He needs that whiskey bottle I saw you put in your little bag this morning."

Angus rolled out the dough carefully with the bottle on the bark sheet. He placed one deftly in the greased bottom of the largest frying pan. When the men gave him their blueberries, he put their berries in the pan, sprinkled them with sugar, and then put the other dough on top. Alternately propping the pan against the fire and holding it over, the pie was soon done.

Chapter Two

I

"We have to find Shane, Edith," the priest insisted.

The Cree woman said nothing. She looked uncomfortably at the floor.

The priest hesitated. He knew it was no use speaking long to the woman. He had already explained to her why her little six-year-old son had to go to residential school in North Bay. It was good for him to receive an education.

Edith Bearskin lived on the reservation in Moose Factory, an island in the mouth of the Moose River not far from James Bay. Her small house was government-constructed, plain, standardized, but with electricity. Now, as she listened to the priest, she repaired a large fish net in the kitchen and kept one eye on the pot on the stove. She had just put smoked moose meat in the pot to make stew.

"Where is he?" the priest asked.

"He went in the woods," she said.

"Do you know where he went?" the priest asked.

The woman said nothing. The priest suspected that her silence meant that she had some idea of the little boy's whereabouts.

"When did he go?"

"Last night, I think," she said.

"Last night!" the priest exclaimed. "He's only six years old."

"He's been in the woods by himself before."

"I'm going to have to ask your brother to go find him. It's nine o'clock. The train for North Bay leaves at four this afternoon."

Edith's brother found little Shane within two hours.

II

Shane was tall for his age, but he still had a baby face. His pudgy cheeks and high cheekbones crowded his eyes into slits. When he laughed, as he often did, the eyes virtually closed. His close-cropped black hair shone in the light from the railcar window as the car rumbled south from James Bay.

"What are they going to do with us?" a frightened little Shane asked his small friend seated next to him in the railcar. He spoke in Cree.

"I don't know," the other little boy said.

The car was full of Indian children, all about the same age, all going to residential school for Indian children in North Bay. The priest from Moose Factory accompanied them. An Indian woman came along as well.

The priest looked at the children, all of whom he knew. Then he spoke to the Indian woman, who did church work for him.

"You know," he said, and there was a sadness in his voice, "I'm not happy about this." The priest was speaking in Cree, though quietly, so the children would not overhear.

The woman nodded in agreement.

The priest went on in Cree. "These are happy children. At least, they're happy in Moose Factory. They're not happy here." He looked at all the sad faces. In any other circumstances, any other place, doing any other thing, there would be happy Indian children before him.

The woman's silence showed her sympathy with what he was saying.

"If you would have told me that I could wipe the smiles from the faces of thirty Indian children, all at the same time, I would not have believed it."

The train chugged along the Abitibi River in the August twilight. Those gazing out of the railcar could see an endless azure carpet of blueberries along the tracks and into the woods.

The priest continued thinking aloud. "These kids get so excited when they're visiting Moosonee and the train comes in. If they were on this train for any other reason than to spend nine months in North Bay at the school, they'd be bubbling."

They rode in silence for a time. The priest went up and down the aisle, trying to raise some cheer in the children. He had no luck. He asked the woman whether she'd like a tea. When she said yes, he poured tea for both of them from his thermos bottle.

He had learned the Cree language at the seminary. He practiced it in years of hard study at Moose Factory. Now he preferred to speak in the language because of the beauty that he came to appreciate very much.

"Schooling is good for them. But they don't see that at their age, and they don't feel it. In my mind, I believe it is necessary. In my heart, I feel as sad as they do. Maybe more. Maybe more, when I look at their faces. The happiness that you see on their faces when they're in Moose Factory has made that island a much happier place for me."

The priest had some thoughts that he did not want to communicate to the Cree woman, for fear of making her more discouraged. He had misgivings about the school itself, but he did not want to undercut confidence in the school by voicing them.

The curriculum — a more appropriate word did not come to his mind — was lacking. It was not appropriate in some ways for Indian children, he felt. And then there was Father Earl. Father Earl was not the man to head the residential school. The priest from Moose Factory knew many priests who were good men and whom he respected. Father Earl was not one of those men.

Most of the children — not excited, not playing with each other — managed to sleep through the night on the train to North Bay. The train pulled into the North Bay station in the early morning.

Father Earl met the group of children at the station.

III

"Don't you dare speak Indian! Don't you dare!" the nun shouted at six-year-old Shane. The little boy shrank in his desk just as the nun swung the leather strap. He did not pull his hands back quickly enough to keep the brutal strap from searing them.

"You're the worst one in the class!" the nun exclaimed, nearly hysterical. "I tell you not to speak Indian and you continue to speak it! I'm going to make an example of you!" She stood for a moment trying to catch her breath. She wanted to tell the class that English was God's language — perhaps that would help — but she wasn't absolutely sure that it was, so she might have to go to confession to absolve herself if she said it. But this little Shane insisted on speaking his language, and she would have to make an example of him, or she'd lose the whole class to the Cree language.

There was no way for Shane to tell her that he did not continue to speak Indian only to provoke her. He felt alone at the school, very alone. He did not have his mother. The only ones he had were his little friends. In two months at the school, he knew very few words of English — not enough to speak to his friends. He did not feel so alone when he spoke to them in Indian.

"Now!" the nun said, looking at little Shane cowering in his seat, "Are you going to speak in English only from now on! Answer me! Answer me! Answer me, I tell you!"

Shane, very fearful, trembling, said nothing. In his fear, he felt as though he had lost the power of speech.

His terror mounted as the nun moved even closer to him and drew back the leather strap in wild anger. Now all the children in the room were cringing in fear at what was going to happen to their little friend. "Speak! Speak! Speak!" she shouted. "Tell me that you're going to speak only in English!"

Little Shane looked fearfully at the nun towering above him, and he told her that he would speak English only. He told her in the only language he knew. "*Ningat aganecam eta,*" he said timidly.

The nun exploded, pulling Shane's hands from his torso and whipping them as hard as she could with the leather strap. As the blood covered his little fingers, a flood of tears came to his eyes.

IV

The nun who put the little boys to bed in the same room each night was friendly.

"Now," she said, "you must be quiet and not talk when you go to bed so you can get a good night's sleep. You can visit with your chums in the morning. So you say your night-time prayers and think how much fun it will be to see your friends in the morning."

The little boys dutifully tucked themselves under the covers of their beds after they had knelt by the beds for prayers.

Before the nun turned the lights off, she smiled and said, "Always remember what I told you about not drinking any water after supper. It's no fun to have to go to the bathroom in the middle of the night."

But Shane had drunk water after supper, and he did have to go to the bathroom in the dark, something he did not enjoy.

Late at night, Shane rose from his little bed and walked quietly to the large boys' bathroom. He wasn't afraid in the woods in the dark, but this big, old, sepulchral school building was something else. He'd heard of ghosts, doubted they were in the woods, but he wouldn't be surprised if they haunted old, dark buildings like this one. He turned on the light in the bathroom and walked to a urinal. Just as he opened the fly to his pyjama bottoms, he heard footsteps on the other side of the door. Adult footsteps. The door opened slowly. It was Father Earl.

Shane was nervous; the urine would not come. He expected Father Earl to scold him, but it was just the opposite. "Well, Shane," the priest said. "Got to go tinkle in the middle of the night, eh? Here, let me help you." He walked towards Shane.

Shane, still unable to urinate, looked first to one side and then to the other. Just as the priest was about to touch him, he darted around him to the right, ran through the door back to his bed and pulled the covers over his head, his heart pounding rapidly.

After some minutes, when he felt his heart beating more slowly, he peeked with one eye out from the covers. Father Earl was standing, backlit, in the doorway to the dormitory. The priest turned and walked away.

Some days later, the boy in the next bed became distant and uncommunicative. Shane tried to speak to him. Even in Indian, the boy would not answer. Shane tried several times, gently, but he still could get no response from the boy. Shane did not know what had happened to him, nor did he know what to do about it. But he felt that it had something to do with Father Earl.

V

In June, Shane and the other children took the train back to Moose Factory. The priest from Moose Factory was at the North Bay station. Shane felt relieved to see him.

As he rode the train north towards James Bay, he thought about how happy he would be to get back home. His mother was warmth and every good thing he had known. Moose Factory was his home — not North Bay, not the residential school. There was only one cloud that hung over his journey back to his people.

He would have to return to the residential school in August.

Chapter Three

I

The small log cabin at Ottawa Lake was a rude one, though there was a neatness about it. It measured five paces on one side, seven paces on the other. The wall logs were not notched at the corners but were stacked horizontally in six-foot lengths and spiked to eight-foot uprights every six feet. The neat roof was made of second-hand boards over which tar paper had been laid. The windows were single panes of glass set in the window openings with small board frames. The cabin had not cost more than two hundred dollars, yet it gave the impression of having been built with skill.

The cabin was set in a small cove. Tall black spruce, their lower branches cut off, sheltered the cabin. The point that helped to form the cove hid from sight the Ottawa Lake lumber camp, two miles down the lake and on the opposite shore.

Angus Wawati was skinning a beaver inside the cabin. His tool was a short knife with a round, broad, very sharp tip. His skilful strokes sliced the fat and sinew from the pelt without cutting the skin. When he finished, the skin was so clean that it looked as though it had never had fat and sinew attached to it.

His daughter, five-year-old Theresa, was watching him. She was small, with fine little features that looked as though they were done in porcelain. She smiled frequently and when she jumped up and down, her straight, black hair seemed to do so too.

Theresa alternately smiled and talked to her father Angus as he strung the beaver pelt on the round stretching-rack made of alder branches. Occasionally she played with a little wooden toy that her father had made her. Her brother and sister were outside helping their mother tan the hide of a moose that Angus had shot the week before.

The inside of the cabin was simple. There was a wood stove in the middle. A sink under the window drained only to the outside. The water pail was next to it. They fetched the drinking water directly from Ottawa Lake. Angus and his wife had a bed in the corner of the cabin; Theresa and her brother and sister slept together in a smaller bed. Clothes hung on nails, fixed head-high in the wall logs.

It was late October, cool and overcast, with a sky that threatened rain. Theresa's mother had lashed the moose hide out on the huge hardwood rack to stretch and dry as she beat it with a hardwood club. Now the rain started; she laughed at Theresa and said that she'd go no farther with her work today. Next time she was able to work the hide, she would once again have to wring it out and then begin the stretching, drying, and beating process. For the time being, it would soak in the October rain.

"Help me make supper," Theresa's mother said to her in Algonquin. "Will you go get the moose meat from the spring?"

And Theresa walked off, smiling proudly that her mother asked her to help with the supper. Her little brother and sister were playing by the water's edge, pretending that they were fishing. "Come in out of the rain!" their mother called to them and, laughing, they ran into the cabin.

Theresa's mother used the large butcher knife to slice slabs of moose meat from the big chunk that Theresa had brought in from the spring. *"Ki ta pakwejiganike,"* her mother said to her. Theresa was thrilled that her mother would rely on her to make the bannock. Along with the woods and the animals, her mother and father were all of the world she knew. Her mother relied on her to do things, important things, like make bread, though Theresa was only six years old. When her mother finished tanning the hide, it was Theresa's job to go into the woods alone to gather punk wood in a pack. Sometimes the punk wood had to be poplar; sometimes it had to be cedar, depending upon the colour Theresa's mother wanted the hide to be. Theresa was responsible for knowing which was which because the smoking of the hide was very important. She took her brother and sister with her so they could learn, and the two little ones then thought they were grown up.

Angus Wawati was gone during the summer months to guide for white fishermen at Brascoupé Hunting and Fishing Club, far from Ottawa Lake. He hitched a ride with a lumber truck down the bush road more than a hundred miles to his guiding job. Because of the difficulty of coming and going, Angus remained guiding all summer, only to return to his cabin and family on Ottawa Lake for the fall trapping season and the winter.

"Is it today that the white man — the fur buyer — will come?" Angus's wife asked him. She was beginning to fry the moose meat in a large pan; Theresa had the big bannock loaf frying in another large frying pan alongside.

Angus was stretching a beaver pelt on the small drying-frame. The fur buyer would take only the beaver pelts that had already been stretched and dried. "He said he would come today."

"Will he stay with us?" his wife asked.

"No, I think he'll stay in his truck on the other side of the lake."

II

Supper was finished. Angus and his wife were drinking tea. The three children were playing on their bed. They were playing with the Sears catalogue that Angus had found. He had cut out photos of the models in clothes; those were their dolls.

The quiet rain fell gently upon the waveless lake. The warmth of the wood stove took out any chill in the air inside the cabin. The only sounds within were of the children playing and the fire burning in the stove.

Angus's wife looked up at a sound from the outside. "*Wabickiwe ani tagocin*," she told her husband. The white man is arriving. The children stopped playing, and all could hear from the outside the sounds of the fur buyer's canoe being pulled up on the shore, followed by the clunking of the man's gear in the canoe as he removed his things.

The man entered with two large packsacks. He was short, stocky, watchful. Angus shook his hand. The man started speaking in the white man's language. Angus understood only a handful of words in the language, Theresa not even one. The children sat on the bed now. They had become intensely shy at the arrival of the foreigner.

The fur buyer smiled continuously at Angus. Angus asked his wife to pour the tea. The man put out his hand to the cups as a sign for her not to do so. He reached in one of his packs and took out a bottle of whiskey. He poured the whiskey into Angus's cup and into his own. Soon Angus was more animated than he had been.

After a time, Angus motioned to his wife to follow him outside. They went in back of their cabin to the little shed where he kept the furs. They came back with armloads of furs and set them on the floor of the cabin near the fur buyer.

There were several stacks of stretched beaver pelts, two lynx, a few score marten, and some fisher. The fur buyer counted all of them, examined the quality from time to time, and scratched little figures on a paper with a pencil. Some trappers were sloppy in skinning animals; Angus was the most skilled and meticulous trapper he knew. After he was done counting the pelts, he took from his pack three big bottles of whiskey, set them on the table prominently before Angus, then took some money from his billfold and gave it to him.

Angus asked the man if he wanted to spend the night. No, the man said, he would go back across the lake in the canoe and spend the night in his truck. He had set a bed up there.

III

Angus was throwing things. The children were terrified. The three of them desperately crawled under their little bed after they were hit by thrown objects. They held each other under the bed and cried together. Angus had punched his wife. She was crying, but she was lying on their bed. Theresa called to her mother, "Hurry up and get under your bed, Mommy! Hurry up and get under the bed! You won't get hurt!" But the woman could not crawl under the bed.

Theresa tried to keep her little brother and sister from being terrified, but she was terrified herself. She loved her father, Angus, very much, but this seemed like a different man. Her father was the one who always smiled at her, who made birch-bark baskets just for her, who made wooden toys for all the children. He helped take care of them when they were sick. He took them in the canoe with him. She could remember how much her father liked it when she would walk up to him and watch him and talk to him when he was making a paddle, or repairing snowshoes, or stretching a hide. She could see that he really liked her to be with him.

What had happened now? What had happened to her father and her family? Why did they have to live through this terror? Would they live through this terror?

Crowded under the low bed, she held her crying, terrified little sister and brother to her until they finally went to sleep.

Chapter Four

I

"Do you think an Indian could live in the woods today like the people did long ago?" Jim Gull asked.

"I don't know," Shane Bearskin said, "I think so."

They were sitting in the kitchen of the apartment they shared in an old section of Montreal. Both were in their mid-twenties and both were Cree; Shane Bearskin was from Moose Factory at the southern end of James Bay, and Jim Gull was from Attawapiskat on the eastern shore of the bay.

"But if Indians had to do without guns and steel knives and snowmobiles?" Jim questioned.

"Indians in Moose Factory have all those things, but they still have all the old skills too. It would just be a matter of their adjusting a little bit." Shane offered some tea to Jim before he continued. "I don't want to live in a town. I want to go to the woods. I would not want to feel that I had to go into the woods draped in smoke-tanned moose hide. But I need to be there."

Shane was making supper — fried bologna and potatoes. Jim loved to eat; he lived to eat, thought Shane. Neither was particularly good at washing dishes.

Jim Gull's family name was from the Indian word for gull — *kiock*. The people long ago on James Bay had given this name to Jim's ancestor. The ancestor was always anxious for food, and even sometimes seemed to call for food like a gull: "*Hiyak, hiyah, hiyah!*" Jim did the same.

Shane Bearskin was amazed to see that this trait could be handed down. Every time Shane fixed food in the kitchen, Jim hovered around like a gull, picking at a salad or snitching at pork frying in the pan. It reminded Shane of the gulls that flew circles around Indians' fish nets that were set in the rivers flowing into James Bay.

The apartment was small, with only one bedroom. When he and Jim had moved in, they had flipped a coin to see who would have the small bedroom. Jim had won, so Shane slept on the foldaway couch.

Jim Gull was doing graduate work in biology. Although Shane Bearskin was in his last year of undergraduate work, he was older than Jim, having worked in Moose Factory for some time before he began college.

Jim was tolerant and attentive, the two qualities Shane felt, when he thought about it, were perhaps the most important in a friend. Shane liked him for his ability to fix his attention on whatever was being said in conversation. He always remembered what was said and was able to recall it later. Jim had friends because he was a listener. He was possessed of that rare trait of never deprecating a person behind his back. No sooner did he meet someone than he would be touting that person to a third party. He somehow found something of interest in everyone and spread the information.

Shane had dark good looks. But they were the kind of dark good looks that could have been southern European, to such an extent that the admixture of white blood in his ancestry tempered his Indian physiognomy. His black hair fell to his shoulders. He was sinewy, but muscled, with a narrow waist and broad shoulders.

II

"You look a little down," Jim said to Shane, who was now at the refrigerator putting the canned milk back in. "Is it Theresa again?"

"Yeah."

"What is it this time? A fight?"

"I guess you could call it a spat. But it's the same thing over and over. She's really in love with me, you know. She's so happy when we're together. But she needs so much reinforcement. She's watching everything I do and say to see if I love her. Something positive and she's enraptured."

"I notice you bring her flowers often — more than any other man would," Jim said.

Shane smiled at the thought of how thankfully Theresa always received such gifts. "You give her something and it's as if she forgot everything around her and all the past and just focused on that moment. And her whole life for that instant is full of happiness and joy. She honours the giver by her appreciation. "

"So what causes the problems?" Jim asked.

"It's probably me, when you come right down to it. If she thinks I'm behaving coolly, she gets despondent and that's when the uncomfortableness starts. I'm powerless to stop it. You know, sometimes I think that if I did something truly horrible, it would create less of a problem. She'd probably be very understanding. But let her sense what she feels is a little coolness, and she gets very hard-headed."

"Does she like to fight?"

"Not really, but she does not back down from one. I think it gets going because she's sensitive to the least lack of attention. She's dependent on my affection for her."

"That makes it hard for you," Jim said. Impatient for supper, he rose and went over to the frying pan and picked at the bologna.

"Well, I don't know," Shane answered. "Sure it's hard, but on the other hand, it kind of gives me a little security too; makes me feel wanted, and that at least I'm the most important person in the world to someone."

"She seems to thrive on affection," Jim said.

"I suppose we would too if we'd gone through what she's gone through," Shane responded.

Jim said, "Things weren't all that easy at Moose Factory."

"No, they weren't," Shane agreed. "My dad ran away on my mother, and she had to raise us. But we had it easy compared to Theresa." By way of illustration, he asked, "Do the people at Attawapiskat eat lard sandwiches — two pieces of bread with lard and salt?"

Jim said, "The old people still do."

"Theresa's natural mother at Ottawa Lake used to make them; they had so little to eat sometimes. Once Theresa and I were out getting yellow birch for snowshoes. She made herself a lard sandwich — I don't like them — and she said simply, I'd rather be eating a lard sandwich with you here than be eating in a fancy restaurant in Montreal."

"You told me before that she was taken from her parents, and that she had her own children taken from her."

"Yeah, she was raised in the woods — at Ottawa Lake," Shane said, naming the big lake three hundred miles north of Montreal that was the headwaters of the Ottawa River. "Her father drank and beat her mother. One night when Theresa was seven years old, it got too much for the mother to take. It was raining hard and the only thing the mother had was a canoe. She put the three children in the canoe and spread a canvas tarp over them. Then she paddled as fast as she could across the lake to the lumber camp to escape the father, who by this time was paddling as fast as he could after them in their second canoe. He was drunk and unable to catch them. That was too bad; I've heard that Angus Wawati was one of the most skilled Algonquin in the woods."

"What happened then?" Jim asked, now chewing on another piece of bologna.

"At the lumber camp, they gave Theresa's mother food and a little money in return for helping out in the kitchen and with the laundry. They let her make a little place for herself and the children in a little shed in back of the camp. The children's aid society finally found out about it and took the three children from her. Each of the three was placed in a separate foster home. Theresa never saw her brother and sister again. That was the last she saw of her mother."

"Rough life," Jim opined in sympathy.

"But can you imagine, with all that trouble, she still manages to remember good times at Ottawa Lake. They were really well there, a nice little cabin on the lake, and Angus could get work guiding and he trapped in the fall. Angus brought a Sears catalogue back from Maniwaki once. The children cut the models out and used them for dolls. They used to go sliding down hills on moose hides, and they'd play with the Indian toboggan her father made. She still laughs today when she thinks of all the fun they had with the dolls they cut out of the Sears catalogue."

"That's harder than we ever had it at Attawapiskat," Jim said.

"It got rougher after that," Shane said, "She was raised by a white family in Montreal."

"Too bad she couldn't have grown up with another Indian family," Jim said.

Shane agreed. "They didn't do things like that back then. They took the Indian child out of the environment as soon as they could. The problem might have been with one family, but the social worker looked down on the entire environment: the people and the woods. Today Theresa's caught between the old life in the woods that she remembers and the life in the white world, which for her means being a lawyer so she can help Indians."

"That's what was rougher than being taken from her parents — being raised by a white family?" Jim probed.

"No, I didn't finish. Theresa left the family to work and go to school when she was eighteen. She became pregnant twice and ended up having two children. She loved the children very much. I think they made up the family she never had. Those two children were taken from her and she never saw them again."

"Why?"

"Well," Shane said slowly, "she was a young single mother with no well-paying job skill that she could market. According to what the social worker told me, she had a hard time making ends meet with the children, and drinking finally caused the children to be taken away from her. At least that was the explanation the social worker gave me. She'll never see her children again."

"I don't know how she can accept that," Jim said.

"In her heart, I suppose, she'll never accept it."

They were quiet for a while.

Finally Shane said, "Theresa seems to get along well. In fact, I think she can be quite happy with me most of the time."

Shane rose, walked to the stove to fetch the teapot, and poured some more tea. He brought the frying pan to the table and dished up the fried bologna and potatoes for both of them.

Shane cut the bologna with his fork and ate a piece. He said to Jim, "What do you think of white people?"

Jim ate the bologna and gave himself a few moments to think. "Well," he said after a time, "I think the race has a lot going for it. But despite that, the men are often arrogant and aggressive."

"It's the white women and children I find sad," Shane inserted. "The women are unattractive as women because they are so demanding, and they talk too much. But the saddest thing is the white children. They don't smile enough. Instead of being allowed to be a child, a white five-year-old is trained to be glib and competent."

"Can I brag about Indians?" Jim Gull asked.

Shane Bearskin said, "Nobody will ever hear you but me."

"Indians have a grace and courtesy whites will never know."

They ate in silence for a few moments.

"But Indians are always the victims," Jim proffered.

"You noticed that too," Shane said.

Chapter Five

I

Shane had called Theresa and told her he was coming over to her apartment. When he reached the door of the apartment, he knocked lightly and then let himself in. As he entered, he smiled a little in anticipation of seeing her. She usually came around the corner of the kitchen door, a bit shy yet — though she knew him so well — and smiling broadly that he came to visit her.

"Theresa?" he called, not seeing her immediately.

No answer.

He walked through the door of the small kitchen and saw her standing by the end of the counter. She was weeping softly.

"Theresa!" he said. "What is wrong?" He walked up to her and held her and took out his handkerchief to wipe the tears running down her cheeks.

In answer, she looked at a newspaper on the small kitchen table.

Shane went over to pick it up. It was open to one of the inside pages. Broad headlines across the top of the page read: "Young Native Women to Fast to Death on Parliament Hill." Shane read the article quickly.

The federal government was planning to make drastic cuts in native educational funding. Those Indians already in university would have a difficult time continuing. And a preliminary study had shown that up to eighty percent of the young Indians who managed to complete secondary school would not be able to go to university because of the proposed cuts.

In response, three young Ojibway women from the Northwestern Ontario reservations of Muskrat Dam, Kasabonika, and Kingfisher Lake had decided something needed to be done. The three had met each other in Thunder Bay, where one was going to university and the other two were secretaries.

They had taken a bus from Thunder Bay to Ottawa and had set up a tent on the lawn in front of Parliament. Drinking only Labrador tea, they were going to fast to the death. The Royal Canadian Mounted Police, so quick to remove other protesters from the grounds of Parliament, knew it was politically impossible to forcibly remove these girls.

Shane put the paper down and returned to Theresa and put his arm around her. "Do you know them?" he asked.

She shook her head to say that she did not.

Shane felt that Theresa was glad that he could be there for her.

II

He said to Theresa, "Do you want to know why I like you?"

"Yes," she answered, trying to muster enthusiasm.

"Because you're pretty."

She smiled.

"And because you laugh a lot."

She smiled some more.

"And because you look very Indian."

This time her smile spread across her whole face until her pronounced cheekbones appeared even more pronounced, and her almond eyes themselves seemed to close in a smile.

Theresa thrived on love, so that Shane felt that no attention he showed her ever went unappreciated. When he gave her his attention, she reminded him of the trillium in the woods, how one could almost see their growth when the sun shone after a spring rain.

III

Theresa bought a new blouse.

"What do you think of it?" she asked Shane.

As she showed it to him, she unconsciously rose on her tiptoes. In another woman, that would have been a conscious act. With Theresa, it was a kind of shyness. And it charmed Shane.

"After we're married, we should go back to Moose Factory or to Barrière Lake," Shane said.

Shane's place of upbringing — Moose Factory — was not as urban as Theresa's foster home, Montreal. Nor was it as bush-like as Ottawa Lake. It was, rather, a kind of village life that offered frequent access to the woods.

Barrière Lake, in La Vérendrye Wildlife Reserve, was the Algonquin settlement closest to where Theresa had been born at Ottawa Lake. It was about two hundred and fifty miles northwest of Montreal.

"If I get through law school, I need to stay here in Montreal," Theresa said.

"But what about the woods? We talk about how we want to go back in the woods and leave the city."

"I do want to live in the woods," Theresa said.

Shane pointed out, "If we don't do it when we are able, we'll end up making excuses. Look at all the other Indians in Ottawa and Montreal. They come from the north and come to the city and find well-paying jobs and never go back. They get bought off."

"That's not true," said Theresa. "Lots of them go back to their reservations."

"Sorry," admitted Shane. "Many do go back. But some don't, and I just don't want to be one of the ones who stay."

"I don't want to stay any more than you do. But I can't be a lawyer in the woods."

"You know that I'll work here after I get out of university so that you can go to law school, but then I really want to go back to Moose Factory," Shane said.

"I agree with you. You're better off teaching there among Indians than in Montreal. And your family's there," Theresa said.

"You know I'd go to your family…" Shane began, and then he caught himself. "I'd love to go to Barrière Lake, if we could just leave Montreal."

"I don't think white lawyers are the best to have for land claims and problems with the government."

"You can't trust them?" Shane asked.

"No, you can trust a lot of the lawyers working for us — as much as some Indians," Theresa said, "But Indians feel better with Indian lawyers."

"Did you have a lawyer when you lost your kids?" Shane asked delicately.

"Yes, I guess you could call him a lawyer," Theresa said sadly. "He was white and he was supposed to be working for me. He sure seemed like he didn't care much one way or the other though."

Theresa rose and began to make tea. She looked uncomfortable and did not want to discuss any further the last time she had to employ a lawyer.

"Didn't they hire a lawyer at Barrière to help them with the land claim and the hunting rights things?" Shane asked.

"Yes," Theresa said, "He's from Ottawa. That's what Delores said."

"So how are they doing?"

"Well, I guess they're doing all right. Delores says that they might regain exclusive moose hunting rights in La Vérendrye. She doesn't know about the land claim and the ban on clearcutting, whether they are going to achieve that or not."

"Sounds like the white lawyer might not be so bad after all," Shane suggested.

"I don't think it was the white lawyer who did it," said Theresa. "Delores says it was Maurice Papati."

"Is he still chief at Barrière?" Shane asked.

"He's chief again. Someone else was in for a while and they didn't think he did as good a job as Maurice, so they voted the other one out. The government is scared of Maurice."

"I met him once," said Shane. "He is a big man, isn't he?"

"When Maurice is negotiating with the government people, they're nervous just because he's there," Theresa said.

"So the white lawyer really didn't do much?"

"I don't think so. It's really Maurice and the people up there. If Maurice didn't have the guts, and if the people didn't back him up, the government would just roll over them," Theresa said.

"Won't it be too late for you to help them when you get out of law school a few years from now?" Shane asked.

"It might be too late to help them with those issues," Theresa admitted. "They'll probably be settled by then. But there will always be something. The government will never let the Barrière people be. The government will never let any Indian band in Canada be. The government will always be there trying to take something."

Shane smiled to himself at Theresa's seriousness. She of the eternal smile, she who everyone always visualized with the wide, happy face. She wasn't glum now, but when she talked about Indian land claims and Indian rights, there was an unmistakable seriousness about her.

"I think I have to stay here," Theresa said. "I can make contacts with other lawyers in Montreal and Ottawa, and they can help me and I can help Indians."

"Is it worth it?" Shane asked, "When what you really want is to live in the woods?"

"I don't think whites are going to do much for Indians unless they are paid. Who knows how long Indian Affairs is going to continue funding land claims. Everything is money and power."

"If an Indian gets caught up in the white power game," asked Shane, "doesn't he become white?"

"It's what is in your heart that counts and what you think and how you were brought up," Theresa asserted.

"The MacNeils didn't bring you up to be Indian," Shane pointed out, referring to the foster family in Montreal who had raised Theresa from the age of seven to the age of eighteen.

"No, but they couldn't help it."

"That's why I think we should go to Moose Factory or Barrière Lake," Shane offered. "When I receive my degree, I could go up there and teach. Or at least replace one of the white people with degrees. The young people up at Moose Factory don't want to be Indians any more — at least some of them. My grandfather taught me to make Cree snowshoes, and I can teach that and other skills, especially the language." Shane continued to make the exquisite Cree snowshoes of yellow birch and moose hide in his Montreal apartment, finding the wood in the bush north of Montreal and sending for the babiche from his mother in Moose Factory. He had found a ready market — and at a good price — for the handsome snowshoes in Montreal.

"You don't understand, Shane," Theresa said. "You can't trust the white people. They always want to take. Do you know what happened in La Vérendrye Wildlife Reserve a few years ago? It used to be a hunting reserve for Indians only, the ones from Barrière Lake and Grand Lake Victoria. Then the white hunters started pressuring the government to open up La Vérendrye to moose hunting for white people. The Indians didn't want that, and the government was about to support them. But they thought the Indians would cause trouble if they opened it right away.

"So the government went to the Indians at Barrière Lake and Grand Lake Victoria and said, 'Let us open La Vérendrye to white people for moose hunting, and we'll make it a rule that they have to hire Indian guides. There are no jobs now here so this will provide employment for the Indians.' The Indians agreed."

Theresa poured another tea for Shane and then continued.

"That went on for a few years. Every white hunter who was hunting in La Vérendrye was required to have an Indian guide. Then the white hunters said to themselves, 'Why do we need the Indians to show us where the moose are? We know the territory.' I guess they did, because the Indians had led them to the good places. So they clamoured to the government to get rid of the rule. A short time later, white hunters were free to go there on their own. A typical grab by the white people and the white government," Theresa pointed out. "And it happened in the 1970s, not one hundred years ago. It will happen in the 1990s and after the year 2000. Indians are too tolerant."

"But do we really want to be stuck in Montreal in order to make things better?" Shane asked.

"Maybe not," agreed Theresa. "But the whites never let up. They're poachers." She tried to change the subject. "Do you know there are still birch-bark canoe builders at Barrière Lake?"

"That's something I should learn how to do," Shane said, "I don't think they've made birch-bark canoes at Moose Factory since the turn of the century."

"Yes, you should," Theresa agreed. "Everyone says how beautiful your snowshoes are."

"It's not exactly the same kind of work," Shane pointed out. "But you're right; I ought to learn. The suburbs of Montreal are really not the best place to learn to make a birch-bark canoe. We have to go back to the bush."

"I know we do," Theresa said. "But I've got to try to be a lawyer."

"Let's both graduate from university," Shane said, "Then you apply to law school. If you're accepted, I'll work while you go through law school and then when you graduate, we'll see."

Shane and Theresa sometimes had arguments. And sometimes she did not like the things he liked, and occasionally she did not want to do the things he wanted to do. But always he loved her, and always he showed it, so that she knew that she was the most important thing in his life and would always be.

Chapter Six

I

McTavish Street was a quiet avenue in the English-speaking enclave of Notre-Dame-de-Grâce. The area was not as moneyed as the other English-speaking quarter, Westmount. The latter was just west of the downtown area and east of Notre-Dame-de-Grâce. NDG, as it was familiarly called, was a bustling little community. One of the main streets of downtown Montreal, Sherbrooke Street, continued west to become the main street of Notre-Dame-de-Grâce.

The little shops on the street could not compete in quality with the shops downtown but they were patronized by the local people because the prices were lower. Theatres on the street showed the latest American films — except for the repertory theatre, which showed old American films and the occasional European one.

Theresa exited the bus at McTavish. She walked to the MacNeils' house. The house was a modest one set back from the street. Her foster father, Tony MacNeil, was a postman and would be at work. Unless Grace MacNeil was out shopping, she would be home and the back door would be unlocked.

She walked up the driveway and opened the back door and walked in. "Hello, Mom?" she said as she entered through the door.

"Hi, Theresa," Mrs. MacNeil said as she came into the kitchen from the living room. "Gee, maybe you ought to knock before you come in. I never know who it might be."

Theresa was a little taken aback by this, even though she knew it was reasonable. She had never thought of the house as a place where she needed to knock.

"I had to get some things from a library here, so I thought I'd stop in," she said.

"Would you like a tea?" Mrs. MacNeil asked, and waited until Theresa said "yes" before putting the tea kettle on. Though it was twelve-thirty, Mrs. MacNeil made no offer about lunch, nor did she inquire if Theresa had eaten.

"Dad will be home about two-thirty."

"How is he feeling?" Theresa asked.

"He's feeling pretty good," Mrs. MacNeil said. "Walking keeps him young. He's got three years to go at the post office, and I don't think he is looking forward to retirement, because he won't know what to do with himself when he can't go down to the post office every morning. He doesn't know what to do with himself on weekends, so I don't know what I'm going to do with him when he's around here all day, seven days a week. You know how he was when you were at home — no hobbies. If only he had a garden or something. Thank God he's got the post office."

Theresa nodded.

"About all I can get him to do is to fish in the summer and even that is a chore for him. He's in love with his easy chair. I wish Ann wouldn't have given it to him," Mrs. MacNeil said, referring to her natural daughter.

"Does he mind going to see Ann in Ottawa?" Theresa asked.

"No, he likes the trip up there to see Ann and Bill and the children. He likes to drive on the open road; he doesn't like it in the city. Ann's two oldest kids are in school, and Samantha will start school next year. Sure crazy how time flies, isn't it?"

Theresa allowed that it was.

Mrs. MacNeil had set the tea on the table along with some cookies. Theresa took one and began eating it slowly. The kitchen was a homey one with flowers in pots, and there were cookie jars and embroidered decorations of various sorts. In the kitchen and down the hallway, there was an inordinate number of photos — photos of Tony and his wife, Grace; photos of them with Ann at all ages; many photos of Ann by herself; photos of Ann and her husband; of Ann and the children; and of the three children at their various ages. Counting the large display frames that had many photos in each, it seemed to Theresa that there may have been nearly one hundred photos on the walls and tables and countertops. She had grown up with the MacNeils; they were the only family she had now. The fact that there was not a single photo of her was something that Theresa had not mentioned to her "Mom," Mrs. MacNeil. And it was even more painful because she had actually given Grace MacNeil some photos of herself in recent years.

"I'll be finishing classes soon," Theresa said meekly, in a small attempt to turn the conversation in a different direction — hers.

"Oh, what year?" Mrs. MacNeil asked.

Theresa hesitated slightly, a bit hurt. "The last year, Mom. I'm graduating."

"Oh," said Mrs. MacNeil. "Ann only went two years before she met Bill. I wonder if she regrets it. I guess it doesn't matter a lot one way or another. She's happy staying home with the kids and keeping house. She can't go to university now anyway with all those responsibilities. If she wants to go to university, I suppose there's plenty of time when the kids grow up and are on their own. A lot of women do that." Then Mrs. MacNeil went on, "What are you going to do then, work?"

Again Theresa felt a little pang of hurt. She thought she had already told her. "I'm going to law school, Mom."

"Oh, did you pass your entrance test yet?" Grace MacNeil asked.

"No. But I'll be taking it in a few weeks, and I hope I'll pass it."

"You'll probably do all right. Don't they have special admissions deals for Indians?"

The question hurt Theresa. A combination of factors — the debt she owed Mrs. MacNeil for taking her from a desperate situation and raising her, and the fact that the lady had always represented such an authority figure as she was growing up — caused Theresa only to nod slightly and not to press the issue.

"Is Jason going to go to law school too?" Mrs. MacNeil asked.

"Who?"

"Jason."

"I don't know any Jason," Theresa said.

"Your boyfriend," Mrs. MacNeil said.

"Shane, you mean. No, he's finishing university, and then he's going to work while I go to law school, if I get into law school."

Mrs. MacNeil began, "He's from way in the north somewhere..."

"He's Cree," Theresa pointed out, remembering that she had told her "Mom" at least twice where Shane's home was. "He's from Moose Factory on James Bay."

"Ann really didn't know what she wanted to be when she started college," Mrs. MacNeil said, not precisely continuing the train of thought that had just occupied both of them. "She wanted to be a nurse but, you know, she met Bill and you know how those things happen. You know young people. Maybe one day she'll have a chance again. She did well in high school, and I don't think she'd have any problems with university."

"Does she come home often?" Theresa asked.

"Yes. Oh, yes," Mrs. MacNeil said. "A girl like that who's so close to her family. She drives down nearly once a month to see us. It's only two hours from Ottawa. She comes by herself or with Bill and the kids. If he's busy, she's not shy about coming on her own. She loves her family."

Theresa was nodding all this time, respectfully listening to all Mrs. MacNeil cared to say about the subject. But she was hurt. She, and some others, had thought that she and Ann were "like sisters" as they grew up together. Growing up in the family, she had felt close to Ann. She thought Ann had felt close to her.

How could Theresa express in words that she thought she was part of their family? She grew up with Ann. Ann was, in another way of looking at it, the sister who was tragically taken from her because her natural parents could not form a family for them. She longed to be part of the MacNeil family — as she thought she was. She longed to be part of some family. Her natural mother and father had disappeared. Her brother and sister had been placed in foster homes far away and communication with them had been cut. She wanted desperately to bring the subject up with her "Mom," Mrs. MacNeil, but the uncomfortableness of the prospect for the moment prevented it. How does one fish for love? And if one met with some kind of response, would it not be forced and artificial?

She could speak to Shane about her not feeling part of the MacNeil family. He would be more than understanding. He would offer her warmth and comfort about the problem, but he was not Mrs. MacNeil or the MacNeil family; in any case, Shane's distillation of the affair would be that Indian children should not be raised in white families if they require foster care.

Theresa did not know how to broach the subject. Rather she knew that diffidence would inhibit her from speaking about it directly. So she began, "What was it like when I came here?"

"You were the cutest little thing!" Mrs. MacNeil said. Her legs had been bad in recent years, so when she asked Theresa if she wanted more tea, she told Theresa to get it. After Theresa poured them both more tea, she went on.

"There was a column in the *Montreal Star* in those days. It was called 'Today's Child.'" It was about all sorts of kids who were up for adoption."

Theresa listened attentively without saying anything — nodding at what Mrs. MacNeil was saying and sipping her tea and wondering if there were any way that the good woman would wander onto the subject of the place of Theresa in the family today. Theresa felt no more confident than ever of actually being able to bring the sensitive subject up.

Mrs. MacNeil continued, "I used to look in the column once in a while. Ann was seven then. Dad and I never talked about taking another child. But Ann wasn't going to have any brothers and sisters, so in the back of my mind I kind of thought it would be nice if she had a chum. It wasn't any plan I had, and Dad certainly wasn't thinking about adopting anybody."

"What did the article say?" Theresa asked. She felt denuded in a way; she had had a mother and father once, a nice mother and father, and now she had been advertised in the newspaper like a pet dog or cat.

"They were always sad, sometimes real sad. Once in a while, there was a child whose parents got killed in a car accident. But most often, it was a 'family problem.' Sometimes that meant that the father deserted the mother and the children. Sometimes both the father and the mother deserted the children. With the Indians, usually it was some problem related to drinking. Most of the children in the paper were Indians or Negroes. Most of the time they were cute, but lots of times the child would have some handicap or the people would bring the child back when they found out the problems it had."

"What did they have for me?" Theresa asked quietly.

"Well, they said you were a happy little girl with a lot of laughter. That your bad moods were rare and that after one, your smile would always be there. We didn't see how a little girl taken from her mother could be like that, but you were. They gave your age, and they said you were intelligent and well behaved, and that you were up for adoption or foster care for family problems. It was only when I went to the agency that I found out that your father was drinking. At the time, I didn't think that drinking was hereditary."

Theresa took this as a thinly veiled reference to her having lost her own two children because of her drinking.

Mrs. MacNeil went on. "Even at seven, you were the cutest little girl, with those high cheekbones and that round, chubby, smiling face. I would wonder often how you could smile so much in that picture in the paper after all you went through. Indians have that gift, I guess."

As if to confirm that in a backhanded way, Theresa smiled broadly.

"So I thought it over and thought about whether Dad would go along with it. He usually goes along with what I think. Dad was working as a clerk in the furniture store then. He didn't have the salary he had later when he got in at the post office. Children's Aid was giving a monthly allotment then of I forget how much for each child you'd taken in. So we took you, and that extra money helped to clothe Ann and you and to put food on our table, and Ann had a nice little chum in the bargain. Dad sure was surprised when he came home from work that day and saw this scared, chubby little Indian girl sitting on the edge of the couch, afraid to take her coat off."

The conversation had at least helped Theresa understand better her place in the MacNeil family.

Chapter Seven

I

Theresa awoke in her apartment on Delisle Street near the Université de Montréal. She saw the clock across from her bed as she awoke. It was eight o'clock.

The smell of breakfast filled the apartment. Shane was in the kitchen finishing the omelettes. Theresa rose from the bed. She went to the bathroom, washed and combed her hair. The long, black, silky tresses shone in the least amount of light. At least, she thought, her ancestry had given her some advantage over white people.

The table was set with her cloth serviettes. Toast and cantaloupe slices were already on the table. She looked in the kitchen.

"What do you want?" she said tauntingly. "What kind of bribe is this — omelettes, cantaloupe?"

"What's the matter; can't I spoil you one day out of the week?"

"If you wanted to spoil me, you'd make breakfast the other six days too."

"I'm just giving you a little treat because the rest of the day is going to be filled with work," Shane said.

"Work! This is Saturday; neither one of us works."

"That's what you think," said Shane, delighted to be scheming.

"Just what have you got in mind?" Theresa asked.

"I need some yellow birch for some snowshoes. I thought we'd drive up to Saint-Donat and take the bush there and see if we could find some. Want to come?" The question was unnecessary. It was understood that they'd go in the bush together, around Montreal, whenever the pitifully few opportunities to do so presented themselves.

"*Anibicwabo ki wi minikwen na nongom? Kiga madjipiton midjim acitc anibicwabo nopiming abitozang?*" Shane asked.

Theresa tried to understand what he said. "Do I want to... something about tea?"

"Do you want to make some tea now and do you want to bring some food and some tea in the bush at noon?" Shane went on to translate this into her language, Algonquin. "*Ki wi anibicwaboke nongom minawatc ki wi madjipiton midjim acitc anihicwabo nopiming kitci wisiniek abitozang?*"

"What are we ever going to do?" asked Shane.

Theresa thought a minute as she was making the tea. "Either you have to learn Algonquin, or I have to learn Cree."

"Lucky they aren't that far apart," said Shane.

"All the same," Theresa said, "all I recognize are 'tea' and 'drink' from what you said."

"Language is the base of culture," Shane said. "If we can't hang on to that, we don't have much. You were lucky that you left Ottawa Lake only when you were seven so you had the Indian language already." Shane's statement called back memories to Theresa. She could see and she could feel the actual moments of separation from her mother.

"When Mommy knew for sure that we were going to be taken from her, she desperately wanted to give me something of hers to remember her by. She gave me a copy of *Ka Titc Jezos*, the New Testament in Algonquin. Mommy believed in it very much. She made me promise to read it every day."

"Did you?" Shane asked. He was very curious, though he felt slightly ashamed at asking her to recall painful history.

"Yes, I did. Every night. Though through the years I no longer believed in the religious message. But it was the only thing I possessed that belonged to Mommy.

"But I kept that solemn promise to read from it every day. Something very good happened. From reading the book, I learned more of my language, and I had no trouble keeping the Indian I had when we were taken from Mommy. And it was a link to her."

"You're lucky you kept it. It wasn't Momma MacNeil who was going to teach you Algonquin."

"She was nice, I guess, but she wasn't concerned about anything that was Indian," Theresa agreed. "The odd time it even seemed to me that she thought that by raising us in Montreal away from the bush she was saving us from something."

"Are we going to have children?" Shane asked.

Theresa smiled broadly in a way that never failed to charm Shane, no matter what it was she was smiling about. And her laughter was an elixir to him; it became a visceral need.

"The children learn the language of the mother, so I'll learn the language of the mother. We'll both speak Algonquin."

Theresa laughed at how hard working Shane was from then on. "How do you say this? How do you say that?" he went around asking. For the first time, Theresa was obliged to think about her language in detail, and she found it a splendorous thing. An Indian language in the Algonquian linguistic family, it had similarities in grammar and vocabulary to

Cree, in comparison with which it would almost be called a cousin language, as French was to Italian. The two Indian languages were not, however, as closely related as the French in Quebec and the French in France.

"How do you say 'I see the table' and 'I see the tables'?" he asked Theresa, and he was happy to see that there was this further resemblance to Cree, in that both of the Indian languages had a plural verb form when the transitive verb had a plural direct object.

II

Theresa packed the lunch and the tea in the wooden grub box with a tumpline on it. Shane put it in the back of his pick-up truck and then put his chainsaw, his axes, and the wooden wedges and wooden mallet in the box in back.

They entered the Décarie Expressway and headed north. When they were on the Autoroute des Laurentides, they joined a heavy, fast-moving stream of cars on their way up to chalets in the Laurentians for the weekend.

"Cottage country," Shane said.

"Wonderful," said Theresa, with sarcasm.

"We're part of it now and for the foreseeable future," Shane pointed out. "It's pathetic to see these people spend so much money on country cottages, and then have to scrimp for time to get there, just to have a little time in the bush."

"I wish we didn't have to stay here for law school — if I get in," said Theresa.

"You'll get in," Shane assured her. "But we don't have to stay."

"If I get in, I have to stay," Theresa said, determined.

Shane looked at all the new automobiles whizzing past them. For some reason, there seemed to be a greater number of automobiles that were new in Quebec, or at least this part of Quebec, than in other places he had been. "People scrambling to get ahead to have more money, and some day — this is the joke — they think they're going to have more time. You notice how everything is so relaxed at Barrière Lake and at Moose Factory, especially with the old people?"

"Yes, I know," said Theresa.

"That's why I regret the rat race," said Shane. "Just to get more material things."

"You know I am not studying to be a lawyer just to have a fancy office and buy a new car."

"I know that," Shane allowed.

"Then…?"

Shane went on, "I can see how you and I could have money ahead and become caught up in the white man's world as easily as these upward movers passing us on the autoroute."

"I won't."

"I don't think you will, and I don't think I will either," Shane said. "But if we become caught up in this money-hungry game, we wouldn't be the first Indians who did. There are enough living in Ottawa and Montreal."

Theresa let that train of conversation peter out. She reached into her pack and pulled out an audiocassette. She turned on the radio and put the tape in. The tape began playing: "*Kije Manito kigi kljigonan. Kitci mackawiziwin ot aian, Win kakina keko oma oga ojitotc — wakwik aeitc akikak. Kakina dac omagatatamak.*

"*Nitam Kije Manito ogi ojian naben. Ogi ojian dac nasem kidjinazozitc. Nitam nabe Adam ijinikazogoban. Ot okoman Eba inikazogobanen…*"

"What is that?" Shane asked.

"Algonquin."

"Yes, of course it's Algonquin. It sounds like something religious."

"It is," Theresa said. "It's the Old Testament."

"Look. I don't believe in the Old Testament, the New Testament, the Bible or that religion. I had enough of it when I was a kid at Moose Factory."

"I don't believe in it either," Theresa said, "but it was the only cassette I could find in Algonquin. It comes from some missionary group in California."

"Well, if that's all we have. We should record some of the old people at Barrière Lake."

"Some of these people are from Barrière Lake — and Grand Lake Victoria and Maniwaki," Theresa pointed out. "Notice the first woman, how clearly she speaks. She's from Grand Lake Victoria."

"Yes," Shane agreed. "But what I mean is that we should record some Barrière Lake people with some bush stories or some stories about the old days. Leave that Bible stuff to other people."

Just the same, he recognized the value of the cassette as a language tool, so they played it over and over again.

III

"Some of the nouns I don't understand, but a lot I do," Shane said, and he asked her the meaning of a few. "A lot of things I can almost piece together."

"You'll get it," Theresa said. "We'll keep at it, and then we'll be speaking Algonquin well if we ever have children."

Shane knew she wanted more children, and he very much wanted to have children with her. After playing the cassette several times, she turned it off and they continued their way up the autoroute through Sainte-Adèle, Val Morin, and the other small, sleepy Laurentian towns that had now become fashionable as ski resorts and centres for the chalet crowd.

He broached the subject that he knew was very sensitive for her, but as important to her as it was to him.

"Do you miss your children?" he asked gently.

And it seemed as soon as the last syllable reached her ears, her eyes welled up with tears. Shane reached across the seat, pulled her to him and put his arm around her.

With tears flooding her eyes, she began, "I think of them all the time. It's like my heart was torn out every day. You don't know how hard it is."

Driving with one hand, he hugged her as close as he could.

"I thought of suicide, and I still think of it once in a while," she said.

"Don't think like that!" Shane admonished, "We've got each other." Shane was reminded of something Jim Gull had said to him: "Theresa is only looking for one thing in life, a simple thing — someone to love her. I think she's found that in you."

"I know we have each other," she said, "and that's good, but you don't know how much it hurts me to think about the children."

"I can see how it would," Shane said, holding her even closer. "I know you will never forget them, but the pain will lessen with time."

"I don't think it ever can," she said. And she looked out at the forest going by almost as though she saw the faces of her two children in the trees.

Chapter Eight

I

They turned off the highway to Sainte-Agathe. The road now went through country that could be called bush. With the exception of settlers' houses along the secondary road and the chalets and country homes of Montrealers that bordered some lakes and were also along the road, the uncut woods stretched away from the road as far as the horizon in all directions.

The road bridged a stream that was hurrying away with the spring runoff.

Shane and Theresa were looking at the same spot on the stream bank, but it was Shane who said, "Look at that mink with the frog in its mouth."

Theresa saw no more than a dark, sinuous form on the bank. "You see more in the bush than I do," she said with a hint of frustration.

"See the yellow birch up there?" Shane said, pointing to the side of a hill where the yellow birches were interspersed with maples, white birches, and the occasional oak.

"Could we cut one there?" Theresa asked.

"I'd rather not. We'd just get started and some officer of the law would come along and tell us it is not legal to be cutting a tree up here. That's what makes me mad. The companies clear-cut anywhere they feel like it, and an Indian couldn't even take one yellow birch without ending up in jail."

"And it isn't even their land," Theresa said.

"Yeah," said Shane, "They won't let you make bail for pointing that out to them."

II

They drove through the village of Saint-Donat and turned east, away from Mont Tremblant looming to the west. Soon they were on a bush road. They no longer met vehicles.

"We're better off here," said Shane, "on Crown land. If someone gives us a hard time, we can probably talk our way out of it."

He stopped the truck by the side of the road at a spot where some yellow birches hid among some other trees. He took his chainsaw out of the back. Theresa shouldered his packsack containing wooden wedges, axes, and the mallet.

"It's easy to see through the woods now," Theresa said. "The leaves aren't out yet, and you can see the trees far away."

Shane's walking through the woods roused a red squirrel, proprietary of its territory. When the squirrel became angry, a flight of birds, and two small hidden animals, joined in the uproar. The feverish antics of the irritated little squirrel caused Theresa to laugh all the way down to her toes.

As they walked away from the red squirrel and its friends, Theresa bent down and picked a plant. "Oh, look," she said. "Here's some *akoskowewack*." Her almond eyes examined it intently. "What is it called in Cree?"

"I don't know," Shane said, "And I don't know the plant. What is the English name?"

"I don't know," she said, "But it brings love. My mother told me about it long ago."

Shane walked up to several yellow birches in turn, Theresa walking behind him with the packsack. He disqualified one after the other, either because the trunks were slightly crooked or because they had branches.

"It's good to walk in the bush," Theresa said, not the slightest bit out of breath but rather seeming to develop more energy as she followed Shane up and down over the ridges on the flank of the hill. Her braids danced on her shoulders as she walked. "It seems like being in jail to have to stay in Montreal a few more years."

Shane was going to point out that it would not be absolutely necessary. But then, they had been over that before, and she certainly would not want to hear it again.

He finally came up to a yellow birch that was eight inches in diameter and straight, without branches, for at least twelve feet. "*Onicicin*," he said. Theresa was happy to see that he used the Algonquin word for "it is good" rather than the Cree word.

He quickly started the chainsaw and cut the tree down. Then he cut an eight-foot log from near the bottom of the trunk. He propped the top end of the log up slightly so he could begin splitting from that end.

"Can you give me the axe?" Shane said to Theresa, standing near him.

She looked perplexed, which in turn made him perplexed.

"May I have the axe?" he repeated.

She still had an uncomprehending look on her face.

"Oh, sorry," Shane said, realizing the problem at last. "*Wakâkwat ni mämesin.*"

And she handed him the axe. She laughed delightedly at her own joke.

He put the axe head at the centre of the top end of the log. He hit it hard with the wooden mallet. The log began to split. He put one of the wooden wedges in the split. Then he hit it with the wooden mallet. The log split easily. He continued splitting the log into quarters and then into eighths.

Shane stopped working suddenly and stood up. Theresa heard the faraway squealing at the same instant he did. "It's coming from over there," she said, pointing along the flank of the hill that they were on.

They walked through the trees and underbrush, over a small rise, and then into a shallow ravine. "A beaver's been caught in a trap," Shane said, even before they were upon the animal.

The year-old beaver was emitting excruciating squeals. "His paw has been ripped in the trap," Shane said as they approached. They sensed the wariness of other animals at the beaver's showing its formidable pain. "It will chew its paw off if we don't get it out."

He started speaking soothingly to the beaver so that he could approach. "Now, little fellow, you quiet down, and I'll be able to open the trap and let you go."

But the beaver, already in great pain, became ever more anxious at the presence of the big animal that was Shane. "We won't hurt you," Shane said. "Take it easy and calm down, and I'll take the trap off your leg."

Despite Shane's soothing talk, the beaver was still squealing. Shane approached and bent down towards the beaver. He extended his hand slowly in the little beaver's direction. The beaver leapt up toward Shane's hand, snapping his teeth together. His teeth would have taken off one or more of Shane's fingers had not the trap held the beaver back. More than one trapper in Moose Factory had lost a finger to a beaver.

Theresa came up to Shane's side and began speaking quietly to the little beaver. "*Kwe, amikons. Onzsm ki maw. Kiga mino pimatis; wibate kiga pimose wewenint.*" As she continued speaking in Indian, the little beaver began to calm down. Soon he was quiet, and Shane pried the trap open, releasing the beaver and allowing him to amble down the stream bed.

They returned to the yellow birch that had to be split. "I'll go make tea," Theresa announced, and she walked back to the truck and left Shane to finish splitting the log.

She cut a fresh six-foot stick with her axe. She propped it up in the air diagonally with large stones at one end. The end that was up in the air was over the fireplace. She went to a nearby stream and filled a large tin can with water. This she hung on the high end of the cooking stick and over the fireplace. She made the fire and boiled the tea in this.

Shane walked up and sat next to the fire and waited for the tea and lunch.

With a small one-hand bucksaw, Theresa sawed a small dead spruce into two-foot lengths. She laid several side to side in the small fire, and these became the cooking grate that would support her large frying pan. Into the pan, she put cut-up potatoes and onions and sliced bologna.

"How would you like to be one of those fancy lawyers who has lunch every day in the Ritz-Carlton?" Shane asked.

Theresa laughed heartily and then the joyous laugh evolved into a broad smile. "This is fine." And she brushed her long braids back over her shoulders and took a bite of the bologna and sipped her tea. Her gaze slowly panned the leafless woods, as if trying to spot a partridge, a deer or a moose, or whatever would turn up.

"Are there moose or deer here?" she asked Shane.

"Both," he said. "I saw moose scat and a rubbing made by a deer. And you see here…" he snapped the top off a two-foot maple shoot, "… see how the deer have browsed on the new growth."

She took the twig in her hand. Shane always delighted in her curiosity when he pointed something out to her.

"This must be the northern limit of the deer and the southern limit of the moose. You don't often see them together."

They sat for a while, quietly drinking tea and looking at the bush.

"When is your law school examination?" Shane asked.

"Two weeks."

"Are you going to pass?"

And Theresa laughed that happy, abandoned laugh that was part of her way of looking at the world — but that told Shane neither whether she was laughing at the examination because she felt it would be ridiculously easy, nor whether she believed she had no chance whatsoever of passing it.

"Delores said there's going to be another demonstration at Barrière Lake in a few days," Theresa said. "They can't get them to stop clear-cutting and to stop spraying herbicides on wild blueberries. So they're going to put some more pressure on the government."

"What did Delores say they were going to do?"

"She didn't say. She said she couldn't let out information ahead of time, but she said it would help if we were there."

"Are we going?" Shane asked.

"Yes."

When they finished lunch, Shane took a whetstone and honed the axe to a razor edge. Then he returned to the yellow birch log.

Gripping the axe handle next to the head, he held one end of the split yellow birch pieces on his shoulder, the other end on the ground. He shaped each piece with the axe until it was square and about the size of the long stick he would eventually bend to form the snowshoe frame. He partially finished each piece in the woods so that it would be less weight to carry back to the truck and haul back to Montreal.

When he finished forming the pieces, and Theresa had packed up the grub box and axes and wedges, they returned to the truck and started off for Montreal.

Chapter Nine

I

"Something tells me this is going to get ugly," Shane said.

Theresa looked worried.

Shane pulled the truck onto the shoulder of the road behind a line of parked cars, Indians' cars from the looks of them.

"What happened?" Theresa asked.

Shane stood on the front hood of the truck and looked ahead. "This is the bridge at Camatose. I see a backhoe. The Indians must have brought it up from Barrière Lake. They took the dirt from the side of the bank and piled it on the bridge in the middle of the highway. This is going to be interesting — the only highway going north."

Shane and Theresa arrived after the last scoopful of dirt had been dumped on the middle of the road at the bridge. The bridge was the only way to cross the river; there was no ditch. Three or four cars were now stopped on the roadway at the pile, and the stream of traffic assured that scores of cars and trucks would be backed up fast.

It was an unusually hot day for late April.

"The white people are going to love this," Shane said, "There's usually a strong wind blowing over the bridge. There's no air moving now."

"And the mosquitoes are starting to come out," Theresa said. "Let's walk up and see if we can find Delores."

They walked along the line of Indian cars and trucks parked on the shoulder of the road. The line of vehicles backed up on the highway was growing longer by the minute.

"There's Delores!" Theresa exclaimed happily.

Delores was three cars ahead in the line. Just then she turned, saw Theresa and Shane and ran to Theresa and held her.

"Hi!" she said, smiling broadly. She and Theresa smiled happily at each other.

Delores was in her late twenties, had a very pretty face and extremely beautiful black hair. However, the whole effect was much diminished by the fact that she was at least fifty pounds overweight, and her face was severely pockmarked.

"How have you been?" Delores went on happily.

Shane, who some people accused of not smiling enough, could not get over how much Indian women smiled, especially at each other. He was eager to find out what was going on, but the two women continued to stand there and smile at each other.

Finally Theresa asked, "What is happening?"

Delores leaned against the car. "Well, we went down to Ottawa and camped out on Parliament Hill. We had some canvas tents and teepees and stayed there for a few days. We got lots of publicity, hut no results from Parliament or anybody else. But we had a lot of white people on our side when they put pictures in the paper of the RCMP hauling away old Indian women in scarves and long dresses. The minister of Indian Affairs finally came down but he couldn't do anything either. Or maybe he wouldn't do anything."

"Is that why you came here?" Theresa asked.

"Yeah," Delores said. "Maurice said he wanted to increase the pressure."

"Why did he pick the Camatose bridge?" Shane asked.

"Well," began Delores, "because it's convenient; it's close to Barrière Lake; it's easy to shut off the road — they can't get around into any ditch — and Maurice thinks he can put pressure on the government."

Shane looked around and in an instant agreed with Maurice Papati, the chief. The line on the south side of the bridge was now more than half a mile long. As he looked at the end of the file in the distance, he could see six or seven cars and trucks pulling to a stop. Pressure there would be, it was obvious; he just hoped that it did not create a violent reaction. Occasionally, cars honked but when they saw what the situation was, or heard what it was from motorists that had been stopped before them, they stopped honking, left their cars to talk to the other people, and swatted away the mosquitoes to the best of their ability.

"How long does Maurice want to keep the road blocked?" Shane asked.

"He said at least all day," Delores recalled. "It depends a little on what happens. He wants the Indians to hand out flyers to the people telling them what we want. Then they will know what is going on, and the police will hear about it, and the government will know that we can go even further."

Shane saw an Indian passing by with flyers he was handing out to the cars. He motioned for one. He and Theresa read it together silently.

The Barrière Lake Algonquin Band apologized for the great inconvenience that their blocking the bridge caused. They did it because it was necessary that some forceful action be taken quickly — they would do it if the government would not — to protect the natural environment and food resources of the band. They were a band that depended upon the immediate natural environment for sustenance, unlike bands further south who were surrounded by a white culture that had directly appropriated the resources and had even supplanted the Indian culture in those areas.

The flyer went on — one version was in English, the other in French — in simple language to explain exactly what the Barrière Lake band wanted in La Vérendrye Wildlife Reserve.

It explained that the reserve was about one hundred and twenty miles north to south, fifty miles east to west, and that there were no year-long white inhabitants in this area.

The government gave the lumber company cutting rights in this area and then exercised no intelligent supervision over the cutting. The company made vast clear-cuts which the company and the government worked hard to keep from the eyes of the public. Motorists travelling along the main highway in the reserve never saw them. They were at all times hidden by a belt of trees. An offer was made in the flyer to drive any interested motorist one and a half miles from the Camatose Bridge to a place where a clear-cut was at least several miles across.

As part of a rather strange program to plant new trees, the government sprayed strong herbicides on large areas of blueberries in the bush on the reserve. The idea was that these areas were planted with seedlings, and the herbicides were designed to kill competing growth and favour the seedlings. But the herbicides were sprayed on the blueberries (which grew best in cut-over areas) and thereby jeopardized an Indian food source. The blueberries ware also a source of income, as the Barrière Algonquin sold large quantities of them to wholesalers in season.

The wood that sold best on the market was softwood — black spruce, the other spruces, and the various pines. The market was the ravenous appetite the American newspapers seemed to have for newsprint. What that meant, in short, for the area was that some good stands of maple and birch that grew in La Vérendrye were actually unprofitable. Incredulous lumberjacks who couldn't actually believe what they were called to do were told to go into the bush, only three miles from Camatose, and cut healthy birch and maple trees. Whence they would be bulldozed into piles and burned. No firewood from them. No boards. Nothing. The idea was simply to clear the land so softwood seedlings could be planted.

The flyer went on to explain how the government had opened up moose hunting in La Vérendrye to white hunters twenty years before, on the promise that it would be made obligatory for these same hunters to hire Barrière Lake guides, and how after a number of years the government succumbed to the pressure of the white hunters who said that they now knew the territory, and it was not right to require the extra expense of Indian guides. The government gave in. And this meant that the Barrière Lake Algonquin were now competing for meat with white hunters from Pennsylvania, Montreal, and Ottawa. The latter were people who could conveniently supply themselves with meat from the IGA.

The flyer then called for a number of clear objectives: consultation with the Indians over clear-cutting and the spraying of herbicides on wild-blueberry areas, and return of La Vérendrye to the exclusive use of the Indians for the purposes of trapping and hunting, though the white people would still be allowed to fish.

Chapter Ten

I

"Hello," Shane said, as Maurice Papati walked past him in the line of vehicles.

"Hello," the young chief said to Shane. They had met only once, briefly.

Theresa also smiled at the chief. "He's a big man," Shane observed, as Papati walked through the crowd and everyone turned to look at him. More than one took a few steps back. "People think I'm big," said Shane, who was six feet one inch tall and one hundred ninety-five pounds. "That man's a giant."

Though Maurice Papati was only six feet three inches tall and two hundred thirty-five pounds, his big-boned structure and visible strength made him tower over the other men.

"*Salut, Jean-Pierre!*" Papati called, as he walked up to the man rising from the driver's seat of a Sûreté du Québec car.

"*Oui. Maurice. Qu'est-ce qui se passe?*"

"*Une petite démonstration, Jean-Pierre. Ni plus ni moins,*" Papati answered. Maurice Papati spoke with great familiarity with Jean-Pierre Boyer because he knew the Sûreté du Québec sergeant well. Whenever the provincial police had business in the Indian village, they stopped to see Chief Papati first. No sooner did they come to the door than Maurice would ask his wife to put the tea on and to bring

out some bannock. Then he'd invite Jean-Pierre and his partner in and, over tea and bannock, they'd discuss whatever
business it was that brought them to the village. And if the
hour were late, Maurice would ask his wife if she would fry
some moose steak. On more than one occasion, when
Maurice made this request of his wife in Indian, he noticed
the two law officers smile broadly as they recognized the only
two words of Alqonquin they knew — *monz wiias*, moose
meat. And it also had happened that Maurice Papati had
gifted Jean-Pierre Boyer more than once with a rather large
portion of moose meat to take home. Which in turn gave
rise to Boyer's habit of bringing a large turkey to the village
on his visits.

"These people," said Boyer, and indicated what was by now
a tremendously long line of cars. "are going to want to kill
somebody."

"*Je sais, Jean-Pierre,*" Maurice averred, "I guess I would too
if I was in the same position."

Jean-Pierre Boyer peered around at the vehicles, then north
across the bridge where there was an equally long line. He
was secretly amused that the Indians had so successfully
fouled up the north-south traffic flow on Highway 117, the
only highway through La Vérendrye.

"We're going to have to do something," Boyer said.

"What?"

"Clear the road, first of all, and then make some arrests,"
the policeman said. "How long had you people originally
figured on blocking the highway?"

Maurice Papati explained, "Long enough to get some
results. Long enough for Québec and Ottawa to understand
that we mean business and that we can do this and more the
next time."

"How long did you think that would be?"

"A day should be enough," Papati said. "After all, there's a lot of traffic on the highway, and we didn't think you'd sit around and let it back up."

"You thought right," said Boyer.

"We need a long enough time to hand out flyers to all these people so they can see our side of the situation, and we need time for the people from the newspapers to get here."

"Who do you expect?" Boyer asked.

"The Montreal and Ottawa papers, UPI, AP, Reuters, Agence France-Presse. Some of them are here already and the rest will be arriving soon," Papati said.

"You people do your homework. The Val d'Or paper wasn't good enough for you?" Boyer asked.

"If you haven't noticed, your government responds only to pressure, not reason or somebody's bad situation. So we will have a little pressure come from outside the country and see what it does. People are sympathetic to Indians in other countries, you know."

Boyer began, "A lot of us are here too. But this is not the way to go about something," he said, and his gaze panned the many scores of vehicles lined up on both sides of the bridge.

"I don't think this will take too long, and I don't mean to make it more painful for everyone than it has to be," Papati said.

"By the way, Maurice," Boyer began, in great clarity so that the chief would get the message, "it's not my job to come here and keep these people quiet while you hand out flyers. It's my job to get this highway opened again."

"I'm not asking you not to do your job," said Maurice.

"No, I know you're not. And I'd like you to help me. I need your backhoe."

"I'd be glad to let you have it. But I've just come from the backhoe. The driver lost the key."

"Christ!" Boyer swore, "It might take me five hours to find one and get it down here from Val d'Or."

"That should be enough time," Maurice observed.

"And then there is the matter of arrests. As soon as I can get some help here, some of you people are going to go to jail."

"Will you do me a favour?" Maurice asked.

"Maurice, if you try to bribe or influence a provincial policeman in the course of his duty, you're going to face a charge a lot more serious than the disturbing-the-peace charge that this is going to bring you. You've been nice to me personally, but I can't let that influence things."

"I know you can't leave here without making an arrest," the chief allowed. "Arrest me. I'm the most visible one here, and the newspapers are going to focus on me. Arrest me and let the others go; and your supervisors will be happy. It will serve no purpose to arrest the others — especially the women and children."

"I can't promise that, Maurice."

The two separated and, given the fact that there was no backhoe or bulldozer to clear the bridge or any other officers to help him with arrests, Jean-Pierre walked up and down the line of traffic, trying to calm passions and reassuring people that equipment was on the way to open up the bridge.

Maurice Papati walked off in the other direction.

Delores was talking and laughing with Theresa. They were standing on the shoulder by the driver's side of Delores's truck, a three-quarter-ton pick-up. A new sports car was parked at the place alongside on the highway. In the sports car were two men dressed in expensive clothes. The driver started up the car and, with several feet of room in front of and behind the vehicle to manoeuver, he backed and advanced until he had taken the car sideways and within three feet of Delores's pick-up.

"Excuse me," the man on the passenger side began, "can you tell me what this demonstration is about?"

"Indians want to have a say in what happens to La Vérendrye," Delores said.

"I gathered that from the flyer," the man said sarcastically. "At first we got kind of mad when we saw how long we were going to be here, but then we got to thinking that maybe we could find a better way to spend our time waiting than just twiddling our thumbs in the car."

Delores and Theresa just looked at the men and wondered what the man had in mind.

"Maybe you'd want to come in the woods with us for a while," the man suggested. "There's a bottle of whiskey in the trunk we could get out."

At this, anything close to a smile vanished from the faces of Delores and Theresa. They turned their backs to the man on the passenger side, though there was little room between the sports car and the big pick-up.

The man put his hand on Theresa and continued, "We could all kind of wander off in the woods for a little while. There's fifty dollars in it for each of you — half now, half later."

Theresa was about to tear herself away from the man's grasp when, over Theresa's shoulder, Delores caught sight of Maurice Papati approaching.

Maurice could not hear what was being said, but he sized up the situation visually. The man on the passenger's side saw, peripherally, an Indian walking up from behind his car and stiffened.

Maurice walked up to the girls and then looked at the truck and the car. He addressed the man on the passenger's side of the sports car. "I think these girls might have some trouble opening the truck door. Excuse me."

He lowered himself between the two vehicles so that his back was braced against the sports car and his boots against the pick-up. He gave a great shove, and the sports car fairly jumped over two feet on the roadway.

The startled man quickly rolled up his window and locked the door as Maurice walked off.

II

Shane and Theresa walked about among the Barrière Lake Indians, seeing people that Theresa knew.

"There are lots of people here," Shane observed.

"They're here for their grandchildren," Theresa said, smiling again as she had before the motorists in the sports car had become obnoxious. She beamed when she saw any of the Barrière Lake Indians she knew.

Shane remembered from Cree mythology the gifts Kitci Manito had bestowed upon his people, and from Christian teachings the gifts God had bestowed upon man, but he thought that the most generous gift that had been bestowed on his people was the gift of laughter, the gift Theresa so freely shared with him and others.

III

The Indians were making almost a festive occasion of it. Grub boxes were open. Fires had been built and tea made.

"*Voulez-vous du thé?*" an old Indian woman asked a few of the motorists who were milling around close to her. A number of them happily accepted the proffered cups of tea. As it was near lunchtime, the woman took out moose meat and started to fry it. Others made bannock. Soon the smell of frying moose meat wafted over the makeshift camp and the line of cars.

A white man approached the Indian women who were cooking by the fire. A woman gave him a cup of tea.

"You people are doing the right thing," he said, smiling and nodding his head in encouragement.

The old Indian woman, in a long dress and with a kerchief on her head, acknowledged his comment with a little nod while still looking at her cooking.

The man glanced at the savoury moose meat in the large pan, now frying in its own juices. He went on smiling. "I'm not saying I wouldn't like to be on my way to Val d'Or, but if I was in your position, I'd be doing the same thing." He glanced at the moose meat again.

"You from Val d'Or?" the old woman asked in heavily accented English.

"No. Montreal," the man answered quickly. "My brother's in Val d'Or; I'm on my way to see him." He was looking at the moose meat.

"The road will be open soon," the old woman said, as she stirred the moose meat in the large frying pan.

The man sipped his tea as he looked at the Indians standing around — and then he looked again at the big frying pan.

The old woman took a large tin plate, filled it with moose meat, and then fetched a big piece of bannock and handed it to the man.

He beamed with enormous pleasure.

IV

Maurice Papati had a piece of moose meat and bannock. He held an empty margarine container full of hot tea. He was sitting on a log not far from the fire. Shane took a plate of food and a cup and went to sit beside him.

"Hello," he said as he sat down by the young chief.

Maurice only nodded in greeting.

Shane became a little uncomfortable. He wanted to speak to Papati, but he did not quite know how to begin the conversation.

It was Maurice who began, "You're Theresa Wawati's boyfriend."

"Yes. I'm from Moose Factory. My name is Shane Bearskin."

"I know some Bearskins from Rupert House and Great Whale River."

"They're cousins of mine," Shane said.

"Theresa's studying law, isn't she?"

"She wants to. She's going to take the entrance examination soon."

"She'll be valuable to the Indians when she gets out of law school." Maurice said. "What are you studying?"

"Psychology. I'm finishing university this spring," Shane said.

"What are you going to do with that?"

"I'm not sure yet. Going back to Moose Factory anyway."

"How do you like our little political-discussion group?" Maurice smiled.

"It seems to be going all right. Do you think it will be effective?"

Maurice went to the fire and picked some more moose meat out of a large frying pan. He poured some more tea and took another piece of bannock. "Nothing is going to change because of today," he said, sitting down on the log again. "But we got people together."

"Is that difficult to do?"

"Yes. Our people were only docile trappers, so the church and the Hudson's Bay Company and Indian Affairs could pretty much tell the Barrière Lake people where to go and what to do and the Indians went along with it. It was hard to get them organized."

"Why are they easier to organize now?" Shane asked.

"It isn't easy," Papati shrugged. "But they can now see that things have to be turned around. The white people passing on the highway don't see the clear-cuts. Our people do because they're in the bush all the time. You don't have to say much to them about what's happening to the moose because they see there are fewer moose here than a few years ago. I don't know how many times I've gone down a bush road and seen some white hunters cutting up a moose. That really affects some of the old Indians, because that means that they may not have enough to eat — at least not enough of the food that they're used to."

"Do you think you can change that?" Shane asked.

"There's a lot we can do," Papati began, taking a sip of his tea. Without the wind, the smoke from the fires was rising and the mosquitoes were eagerly attacking the people. In response, old women were making smudge pots, one of which was set not too far from Maurice Papati for his comfort.

The young chief went on. "We've got the people moving in the same direction. There's even some sympathy outside of the band, which we can mobilize. Now that we're gaining some strength, the government is going to see that."

Just then a few irate motorists began honking their horns. It was as if they thought that if the Indians were forcing them to wait in the heat and mosquitoes, they were not going to allow the Indians to lunch and drink tea in comfort under the shade of trees. The uninterrupted din, which showed no signs of abating, forced Maurice Papati and Shane to stop conversing.

Looking out over the file of cars with their horns blaring, Papati's gaze stopped on a car with four young white men in it. They were wildly making obscene gestures in the direction of the Indians. Maurice set his plate and tea bowl on the log and walked over towards the car.

He stuck his head and shoulders through the window on the driver's side of the car so that the driver had to lean his head back. Then he began politely, "You know, men, I think that if I was in your position, I would get madder than hell too. And I have to tell you that I really don't mind those gestures you're making, under the circumstances, but, ah, I think our women might."

The four men looked at Maurice Papati. They saw his shoulders so broad that they barely fit through the window and his neck so heavily muscled that it actually seemed to be wider than his head. They agreed with him.

As Papati walked back to the log, he saw Jean-Pierre Boyer striding down the line of cars and trucks on the south side of the bridge trying to get the drivers to stop honking.

Just before sitting down, Maurice Papati saw police car lights flashing on the north side of the bridge.

"Come with me," he said to Shane.

They climbed the pile of dirt on the south end of the bridge, walked across and climbed the pile of dirt on the north end. Three Sûreté du Québec cars had pulled up and were flashing their lights. One of the lawmen, the biggest, had jumped out of the lead car and was aggressively addressing the Indians near him. "What the hell do you people think you're doing? My radio's been going nonstop! I'm going to see that all you people go to jail; do you hear that?"

All the Indians were so struck by the officer's tirade that no one answered.

"Who's the goddam head of this powwow anyhow!" he barked.

Maurice Papati then walked up. "I am, officer."

"What the hell do you think you're doing here?" the officer yelled. It was as if he thought he had to yell loud in order to be understood.

"We need this land to live, and we need the meat of the moose to feed us," Maurice Papati said to the provincial policeman.

"Do you have a paper that says that?" the officer asked.

Papati didn't answer, and a highly charged silence followed.

"What's your name!" the SQ man barked finally.

Maurice put out his hand quickly to shake hands, and the officer grabbed it in reflex.

"Maurice Papati. I'm the chief," he said as he shook the officer's hand, and squeezed so hard the big policeman winced. As he continued speaking, Maurice pointed with his left arm south across the bridge, and pulled the big officer around in a semi-circle in the same direction, still shaking his hand. The man was desperately trying to remove his hand from Maurice Papati's vise-like grip.

The young chief continued, "Jean-Pierre Boyer has been here for a couple of hours. Maybe you should go talk to him."

Maurice released the man's hand finally, and the provincial policeman walked across the bridge towards Boyer, flexing his right hand with his left as he did so.

Papati followed the man. As he walked up to where Boyer was talking with the leader of the new contingent, he heard the latter say, "The bulldozer will be here in a few hours, but why don't we start hauling some of these people away? I brought a van, and we have plenty of cars."

Boyer, the senior officer, thought a minute. "You're right," he said. "We can get a little work done while we're waiting for the bulldozer."

He went to his car and took out a pair of handcuffs, then motioned to a patrolman. Then he said to those present, "Papati is responsible for all this. He's the only one we need. We'll lock him up in Val d'Or. Papati, come here," he said, to the surprise and visible disappointment of some of the officers present who would have liked to lock up as many of the Indians as possible.

Maurice Papati stepped up to him and held out his arms. Boyer clamped the handcuffs around his wrists. Then he leaned slightly forward and mumbled quietly to the Algonquin chief, "Pretend these will hold."

Chapter Eleven

I

"Do you have any orders for snowshoes?" Jim Gull asked.

"Three," Shane said, as he worked away with his crooked knife on an eight-foot piece of yellow birch in the small living room of the apartment they shared. The clean yellow birch shavings were starting to pile up on the floor.

"I bet you won't be able to keep up," Jim observed. "Lots of people down here want Cree snowshoes. They are a lot more beautiful than those cowhide contraptions they sell in the sporting goods stores."

"Thanks for the advertisement," Shane said.

"Where are you going to get the babiche?"

"My mother is going to scrape a moose hide in Moose Factory and then send it down to me. I'll cut it up here because I need different thicknesses for the toe, heel, and foot. I'll do that in the basement of the building as I spare you and the landlord the smell."

"Would you teach me how to make the real Cree snowshoes?" Jim asked.

"Sure," Shane said, as he got up to go to his room to get his other crooked knife.

While he was getting set up with another yellow birch stick and a stool for his friend, Jim made a large pot of tea that was intended to last them for a long time.

Jim sat on a stool, facing Shane and carving on the yellow birch piece with his crooked knife. Shane indicated from time to time that Jim should change his grip slightly on the crooked knife for more efficient cutting or hold the yellow birch a little differently for the same reason.

"The crooked knife is not easy on the hand," observed Jim.

"No, but it's a precise tool."

Changing the subject, Jim said, "Do you think Theresa will pass her law school examination?"

"I don't know; I don't know anything about the examination."

"Is it important to her?" Jim asked.

"Yes," Shane said with emphasis. "It's very important to her."

"I thought you two wanted to live in the bush after you're married."

"We do and we will. But Theresa wants to be a lawyer and wants to work for Indians, and she doesn't think she can do that in the bush; she has to be in a city for a while. She thinks the power is in Ottawa or Montreal."

"Maybe she's right," said Jim. "I can't quite see her hanging up a shingle at Ottawa Lake."

"That's the bad part," Shane agreed.

"So how do you go to the bush then?" Jim asked.

"I don't know. Maybe we can build a cabin a hundred miles up in the bush, beyond Sainte-Agathe, and then go there on the weekends. I don't think I'll have any trouble convincing her to take a long vacation once she becomes a lawyer. They've always got a lot of paperwork, and she can just as well do that in a bush cabin and then come back to town. She doesn't want to be around Montreal more than she has to."

II

Theresa had made a supper of fried potatoes with onions, fried moose meat — a gift from friends in Barrière Lake — and carrots and bannock. Shane was eagerly anticipating the meal.

"How long did Maurice Papati stay in jail?" he asked her.

"Delores said he was in jail two weeks," Theresa said.

"Any fine?"

"Five thousand dollars."

"They don't want their roads blocked, do they?" Shane said. "Did they get any concessions from the government on that?"

"Delores said that the government is going to sit down and negotiate all the points."

"Is Maurice happy with that?" Shane asked.

"Delores says that he thinks it's a start, but they are going to keep up the protests while the negotiating is going on."

"Isn't Maurice going to be spending more and more time in jail and paying bigger fines if they continue to block the highway?"

"It looks like they're not going to block the highway any more. They're going to take the problems one by one, work on them individually. For the clear-cutting, they are going to blockade the bush roads so they stop only the loggers and the logging trucks. To get them to stop spraying herbicides on wild blueberries, they are going to find out who the bosses high up in the ministries are and go to Ottawa, Quebec, and Montreal and spray their lawns with manure-based fertilizer.

And for the white hunters who are hunting moose in La Vérendrye, the Indians are mounting loud speakers on top of their pick-ups and they are going to follow the hunters around during the day and at night when they are sleeping, and they're going to play 'O Canada.'"

"Do you think they will be successful?" Shane asked.

"If they keep it up, I suppose. It depends on how the government reacts." Theresa got up to serve more moose meat. "*Ki kitci minopidan monz wiias?* You like moose meat very much. We have to speak more often in Indian."

Shane took a piece of bannock and dipped it in the sauce from the moose meat. He allowed the juice to soak up in the bread before putting it in his mouth and savouring it. "Yes, we need to speak Indian more often and, yes, I like moose meat. Which reminds me, I've got to figure out how I can hunt moose in the Laurentians. We can't keep sponging off our relatives and friends for moose meat."

"They'll make you get a licence," Theresa said.

"Yes," he said, annoyed. "The only place they'll let an Indian hunt without a licence is on a reserve or in La Vérendrye near Barrière Lake or Grand Lake Victoria, and then they want to keep them off the highway so the white people don't see them and complain to the game wardens. If we start hunting north of Montreal, why don't we make a test case of it? Indians shouldn't have to get a licence anywhere, even if they do live off reserves."

"I agree. But we have to have some legal people behind us."

"We know some people in Ottawa and Montreal who could help," Theresa pointed out.

"I'll call them," Shane said.

Theresa picked up the dishes on the table and put them in the sink. She poured them both another cup of tea. Then she looked at him, smiled, and said shyly and sweetly, "Shane?"

"Yes?"

"What's in the box?"

When Shane had arrived some time before, he had brought with him a small cardboard box. The top was folded closed, and there was a small blanket folded up and placed over the top of the box. He had placed it carefully on the living room sofa.

"What makes you think there is something in the box?"

"You're teasing me!" she laughed. "If it was food or something, you would have put it on the counter in the kitchen."

Shane said nonchalantly, "Oh, I'm not really the kind to tease."

"Don't tease me!" she insisted, smiling, and barely able to control her excitement at what it might be.

Shane got up and walked over to the box, picked it up, walked back and placed it in front of Theresa on the table.

Theresa smiled in anticipation as she removed the folded blanket and undid the box flaps.

There in the bottom of the box was a tiny black kitten with big yellow eyes who, just at that moment, after having been silent for more than an hour, gave out a faintly perceptible "meow."

"I thought you might like some company around the apartment," Shane said, happy at watching how Theresa took to the little kitten. The kitten was cupped in her hands and she had the little creature up near her face and was speaking soothingly to it. All at once, the kitten began energetically licking Theresa's face, which in turn delighted Theresa all the more. She placed the kitten on the table, and went to the refrigerator for some milk. Shane couldn't help but look at Theresa. Even when she reached in to get the milk, she was smiling at the thought of her new-found friend. Shane smiled as well. He was happy to be able to

give so little to a young woman who appreciated it so much
— the woman he loved.

"What are you going to name it?" Shane asked.

"Is it a male or a female?" Theresa inquired.

"Female."

"Let me see," Theresa said. "I think I'll call her Annie."

The smile went quickly from Shane's face and he turned
away. "Annie" was the name of the daughter that she had
been forced to give up.

Chapter Twelve

I

How Annie moved, when and what she ate, how she reacted, were important to Theresa. When Annie hopped and jumped for a crumpled paper ball, Theresa experienced great delight. The symbiosis between the two became very real. Shane saw in Theresa a strong nurturing impulse towards everything in the animal world. When Annie hopped at the paper balls, Theresa shrieked and giggled, and that brought joy to him.

"Annie is good company," Theresa said, a few days later, "but I'm going to get some more company."

"What's his name?" asked Shane.

"Don't be silly!" Theresa giggled.

"What's her name then?"

"It's Delores's niece from Barrière Lake. Her name is Victoria, but I only met her once. She got in bad, bad trouble up there."

"She's pregnant?"

Theresa answered him in a tone that suggested that her answer ought to suffice, and that the girl's privacy ought to be respected. "No. Worse."

"How old is she?"

"Nineteen," Theresa answered. "Delores says that she has to get out of Barrière Lake, and that she has to work. So I told her she could stay here, and that I would try to find her a job."

Victoria arrived by bus from Barrière Lake a few days later. Shane and Theresa picked her up at Terminus Voyageur. She was tall, pretty, with high cheekbones and long, lustrous hair and narrow, tranquil eyes. She reminded Shane, all in all, of a younger Theresa, though there was a great difference. Victoria seemed to have experienced some kind of shock — Shane could think of no other word.

Victoria went to the ladies' room at the bus station.

"She's been through something rough," Shane observed.

"Should we have a coffee before we go home?" Theresa said, as a reminder that Victoria's business was Victoria's business.

II

At the meal later in Theresa's apartment, Shane asked, "Would you like some more meat?"

Victoria simply shook her head "no" without saying anything.

Theresa brought some more meat and potatoes to the table and served Shane without trying to engage Victoria in conversation.

Shane avoided trying to speak to Victoria; it seemed to him that she was more likely to talk to Theresa than she was to him.

In the ensuing days, Victoria occasionally was talkative with Theresa, but only in Algonquin. In English, she remained excessively taciturn. She washed her hair frequently and constantly combed it. Then Shane visited Theresa.

Victoria washed the dishes, or in other ways cleaned up around the place, seeming, he thought, to rely on such activity to supplant conversation. She often went into the bedroom when he came to visit.

Once at the dinner table, after having eaten a little, Victoria kept her gaze down. At first Shane thought it was an effort to avoid eye contact with them — and this seemed a rather excessive amount of shyness after having been in the apartment for more than two weeks — but then he saw that her almond eyes were lowered because she was looking at the kitten, Annie, who was sitting in her lap.

III

They were once again heading north along the Autoroute des Laurentides, this time with Jim and Victoria along. Jim was sitting in the cab with Shane. Victoria and Theresa were sitting in the box of the truck. Theresa seemed to enjoy the wind blowing her hair around and watching the Laurentians whiz by. Victoria, on the other hand, was uncommunicative, even to Theresa.

"We should be able to get plenty of yellow birch for both of us," Shane said to Jim. "Then you can make snowshoes all you want. The place we went last time has a fair number of good trees."

"I haven't even finished a pair yet," Jim pointed out.

"It's not all that easy the first time," Shane admitted. "The lacing is especially difficult the first time, even if someone is showing you. You really have to learn to lace the toe, foot, and heel on your own. Someone can 'walk' you through it but to really learn it you have to do the job on your own. It takes me about an hour to lace one snowshoe now. When I was attempting my first snowshoe all by myself, it took me ten hours to lace the first one."

They rode along, with Theresa not trying to talk to Victoria and, in the cab, Shane and Jim talking about various things.

Jim said to Shane: "I noticed that Victoria doesn't say much."

"No," Shane agreed, "she had a pretty rough time of some sort at Barrière Lake."

"What was it?"

"I didn't really try to find out."

"Does she ever say anything?" Jim asked.

"Once in a while, in Theresa's apartment, but I don't try to push her to talk. I sometimes have to ask her something three or four times to get an answer."

"Too bad she's so down," Jim said, "She's a pretty girl."

"That's why I thought going out to Saint-Donat would be good for her. It would get her in the bush with just the four of us and maybe she would relax and feel better."

"If she can't warm up to Theresa, she can't warm up to anyone," Jim observed.

"That's what I think."

IV

Shane pulled up and parked in the bush on the side road where they had earlier harvested the yellow birch for his snowshoe frames.

"The leaves are almost out on the trees now; they were bare when we were here a couple of weeks ago," Shane said. "When the leaves come out, the mosquitoes come out."

Shane and Jim got the chainsaw from the back of the truck, along with the wooden wedges and the wooden mallet. They walked in the bush until they found a suitable yellow birch. Jim mastered the splitting technique quite easily.

While the men were trimming and selecting the best material from the birch, Theresa and Victoria gathered wood for a fire. Though Victoria spoke almost not at all, she did not have to be told to collect firewood, nor what kind of wood it should be.

The fire ready, Theresa cut up a large piece of moose meat into small chunks and then fried the chunks in a very large frying pan. Victoria helped pass the food around but did not speak.

When the meal was done and the yellow birch was loaded in the back of the truck, they all went back to Montreal.

Chapter Thirteen

I

"Delores says that there is an old man from Barrière Lake in Montreal General Hospital."

"Do you know him?" Shane asked.

"No. His name is Thomas Ratt. I don't know him; but I know people in the same family."

They drove down to Montreal General Hospital. They had asked Victoria if she wanted to come along, for she would know the man, and she had said "yes," but almost inaudibly.

The receptionist had sent them up to Thomas Ratt's room. The old man was lying there with his eyes closed. Surrounding him were three old women and an Indian man in his thirties, who had apparently been their driver for the two hundred fifty or so miles from Barrière Lake.

The old women were all short, in their late seventies, though one seemed to be in her eighties. They wore paisley kerchiefs on their heads and long dresses of gingham and plaid that extended down to their ankles. All three wore moccasins on their feet.

Theresa knew none of the Indians there, though Victoria knew them all. Nevertheless, she did not speak to them. Finally, Theresa moved over to the middle-aged man and spoke to him in Indian.

"I'm Theresa Wawati."

The man nodded his head.

"How is Thomas?"

"He's going to die," the man said.

"What kind of sickness does he have?"

"Diabetes."

As they spoke in low voices, Shane understood very little of the Algonquin that they were speaking.

"He's awake?" Theresa asked.

"He's blind," the man said.

"Are these women his sisters?"

"The old one is. The others are his cousins."

The old women stood near the bed. From time to time, one or the other went close to Thomas and put her hand on him for a while. His old sister went up to him and said a few words in Algonquin so quietly that Theresa did not understand. Thomas only made some sort of a low sound. Victoria said nothing to anyone. Shane only stood quietly and regarded the scene.

Theresa, standing back and looking at Thomas, noticed the aroma of smoke-tanned moose hide in the room. His sister, wanting to dress up to visit her dying brother, had put on her best pair of moccasins, a new pair of smoke-tanned ones that still retained the rich, sweet smell of the punk cedar. The aroma of the Indian-tanned hide took Theresa away from the dying Indian's room in Montreal General Hospital, in the great white man's city, and transported her back — long ago and far away — to the bush near Ottawa Lake when she was a child.

It reminded her of her grandmother's deathbed in the little one-room log cabin that her father had made in the bush. There had been the aroma of smoke-tanned hide there. But the aroma also served to remind her of her entire Indian childhood — picking blueberries in vast reaches of the forest when the understory was nearly blue with the fruit; going out in a canoe to help her parents raise a net full of whitefish, walleye, and northern pike, then helping her mother clean them; the excitement that reigned over the camp when her father returned with a moose, and her mother would quickly skin the animal, butcher it and even get from the head such edibles as the nose, tongue, brain and eyes. And it reminded Theresa of helping her mother scrape the hide and then tan it and smoke it. And there was the hanging cradle, made of ropes and a blanket that her father fashioned for the baby. Her mother would push the little hammock back and forth and rock the baby to sleep while she sang quietly. The olfactory sensation of the smoke-tanned moccasins worn by the old woman brought back many memories of times she hadn't thought about for years.

"Too bad he has to die here," Theresa said quietly to Shane.

Shane said nothing but only looked at the poor old man and the old women who had come to see him. But he felt that Thomas was at peace.

The three of them left the room and walked down the corridor. "When I die," said Shane, looking ahead of them down the corridor, "I want people like that around me."

II

One day the telephone rang. Shane had come home from university and was starting to work on his snowshoes. It was Theresa.

"Victoria's got a job!"

"Good!" said Shane. "Where?"

"She was real lucky. It's only about three blocks from here. She won't feel so alone if it's near the apartment."

"What's she doing?" Shane asked.

"She's working for a husband and wife who are both university professors. They've got a little two-year-old girl, and Victoria's going to keep house and take care of the girl."

"Sounds good," said Shane, "maybe it will help her come out of her shell."

"She says it's a nice big house, and the little girl is easy to take care of. The mother and father teach anthropology, and they like Indians," Theresa said.

A few days later the telephone rang in Shane's apartment. It was Theresa. "Are you working on your snowshoes?"

"Yes."

"Victoria gave up her job."

"Why?"

"I told her to quit."

"You told her to quit?" Shane asked.

"The man and woman teachers had different schedules. The man didn't have classes all day. He thought Victoria would make a good girlfriend."

III

"You look nervous," Shane observed a few days later as they walked through Old Montreal.

Theresa didn't say anything immediately, but rather smiled a bit apprehensively. It was raining and Shane was trying to shield her from getting wet. But the rain seemed to keep the other pedestrians indoors and allowed them to be alone on their favourite walk in the large city. Theresa hugged him as if to say that the rain did not matter to her, only being with him did.

"Now what are you so nervous about?" he asked.

"The law school entrance test."

"Well, if you've studied for it…"

"There's only so much you can study for it," she said, "that's the problem."

"You'll do all right," Shane said, as he hugged her.

And Theresa thought that if she did not do well, she had something to fall back on — Shane's love for her.

Theresa had been the only Indian in the law school entrance-test room. There were few women, no blacks, and not many Anglophones. She retained her apprehension all through the test, though she did not find it as difficult as she had feared.

Nor did her nervousness abate, in the days that followed, while she waited for the results.

"I just had a strange telephone call," Theresa phoned Shane one day. "It came from the office of the dean of the law school."

"Maybe this means that you passed."

"It's strange because he wants to see me."

"Is that the way it's usually done?" asked Shane.

"No. The results are sent through the mail." Which in turn made Theresa all the more apprehensive. "Maybe they want to give me the booby prize." And she laughed heartily over the telephone despite her nervousness.

IV

The office of Pierre-Georges de Gaspé, dean of the Faculté de Droit of the Université de Montréal, was on the top floor of the law school. The corner office overlooked the central area of the very large university campus.

Theresa entered the receptionist's area in the very august-looking office. The courteous receptionist rang Dean de Gaspé and then ushered Theresa into the man's office.

The office looked like a law library with hundreds of legal volumes of various sorts, and in several languages, on shelves that went around three walls of the office. The dean was sitting in a very large, leather-upholstered chair behind a grand desk. He rose when Theresa entered.

"Theresa Wawati," he said, extending his hand. "Please be seated," he said, motioning to the chair in front of his desk. "I'm pleased to meet you. Would you care for a cup of coffee?"

Theresa nodded that she would. Whatever it was that he was going to tell her, she wished that he would get on with it.

"Is your last name an Indian name?" he asked.

"Yes," Theresa said.

The dean liked her avid and ingratiating smile, but he could see that she was nervous. "May I ask what it means?"

"It means 'northern lights' in Indian."

"That is quite lovely. I've often felt that the Indian language must be a beautiful language, though I certainly know nothing of it — beyond the fact that many of our place names, like Chicoutimi or Mistassini, come from Indian. Do you speak your language?"

"Yes," Theresa said. She was getting somewhat impatient with the small talk and did not see where it was going to lead, and she was too shy to try to direct it on another tack.

"You're a very well-groomed and attractive young woman," the dean said.

Theresa wondered if he expected something else when an Indian visited.

Dean de Gaspé brought the coffee-serving tray to Theresa. She took a cup. Though the aroma attracted her, she worried that the caffeine in her system would make her even more nervous than she already was.

Were it not for her inevitable politeness and tolerance, her ability to listen to someone talk at length, Theresa would have blurted out that she was curious to know how she had done on the entrance examination.

"Our faculty is a well-respected one, as you know," Dean de Gaspé began. "I don't think I could be accused of conceit if I rated it as the top faculty in North America for French civil law. So while we have many things of which we can boast, we have some problems as well, as all law faculties do. One of our major problems at the moment is that we do not have significant participation by minorities. Do you personally know any Indian lawyers?"

"Two in Ottawa," Theresa said.

"Well, that's two more than I know," the dean said, "and those two must constitute a high percentage of all the native lawyers in Canada. Here at the Université de Montréal, we'd like to help rectify that."

Theresa wondered whether this meant that she would be in on the rectification, or was the dean trying to tell her that she did not make it in spite of all the efforts of the Faculté to give opportunities to Indians? The coffee was indeed making her more nervous.

The dean continued. "Two years ago at the Faculté, we instituted a policy of giving special consideration to natives and to other minorities. By the way, would you like another cup of coffee?"

Theresa was now nervous because of the caffeine, but in her nervousness, she said "yes."

"The program has been working fairly well," Dean de Gaspé said, as he finished pouring her coffee. "That is, with respect to other minorities, such as blacks and certain classes of recent immigrants. But it hasn't really worked with natives for the simple fact that no native has applied in the last two years. That is why I was so glad to see your application."

A white woman in this position would have said something to hurry the dean along in some way, but Theresa just sat there, waiting patiently for him to come to the point.

"Naturally my interest was piqued when I was told that you were to be taking the test. When your test was finished, I asked to have it examined immediately. The way our program works for minority admissions is that the test is only one of several factors that is considered — this is true for the other students as well — but minorities receive an actual numerical increment on their score which is designed to help them in competition with the other students."

Theresa still had no intimation of what her own results were.

"I asked you to come here because there is something I would like to tell you."

Theresa was by now wide-eyed with anticipation. She had a big smile — but a smile of apprehension.

The dean was smiling as he spoke, "You performed quite well on the entrance test. You passed it and, furthermore, you passed it without the bonus we accord to minorities. I hope you'll enjoy your three years at the Faculté de Droit."

Chapter Fourteen

I

"Jim, did Theresa call?" Shane asked as he came into their apartment.

Jim called out from the kitchen. "No, was she supposed to?"

"She said she'd call sometime after one in the afternoon and now it's after three."

"Maybe she forgot."

"She doesn't forget things like that."

Shane called Theresa's apartment, and Victoria answered. Theresa hadn't come by or called in the afternoon.

Shane began pacing back and forth across the living room floor. Jim noticed his nervousness and tried to change the subject. "That was quite something that Theresa got accepted into law school."

"It sure was," Shane answered. "She was really excited. I've never seen her so happy. Do you know what she said to me? She said, 'At least one thing finally went right in my life.'"

Jim shook his head in a combination of agreement and amazement. "Yes, one thing finally did go right. That girl had more hard luck by the time she was seven than you and I will have in our lifetimes."

"Probably," Shane agreed.

"She's wrong about getting admitted to law school being the only thing that has gone right in her life though," Jim said.

"Oh?"

"There's you. If a woman — or anyone — has just one person on the whole earth who loves him as much as you love Theresa, he or she has life licked. Nobody has a right to hope for anything more."

"Thanks, Jim."

Shane continued to pace the living room despite Jim's best efforts to assuage his nervousness.

"You know, two hours is not a helluva lot of time," Jim said. "She forgot or she got busy."

"She doesn't really forget things like that," Shane said, repeating himself from before.

"Two hours late doesn't mean that she's been hit by a car crossing the street," said Jim, immediately thinking that perhaps he could have used a better example to reassure his friend.

Shane dialed Theresa's apartment again, despite the fact that it was only thirty-five minutes since he last called. Victoria said Theresa hadn't called.

Shane put some water on the stove to boil for tea. And while he did so, he paced the living-room floor.

Before he had the tea ready, he got on the telephone. He called Mrs. MacNeil; he called the Faculté de Droit; he called Indian Affairs in Montreal where she knew some people. He called Victoria back, asked if Theresa had, by chance, come in or called, and then he asked if Victoria knew of anyone Theresa knew in Montreal. She did not.

"Where does she go if she's downtown?" Jim asked.

"She goes to one or the other of the English-language bookstores once in a while."

They both had the same thought; should Shane or should he not walk the downtown area and see if they could find her — either in the bookstores or in some of the other places she occasionally visited?

Shane's thoughts started getting a little more disjointed. "Maybe she went for a walk in Old Montreal. She always liked it when we took walks down there."

Jim jumped up to grab the tea kettle off the stove as it was starting to whistle. "Yeah, but in the middle of the afternoon, by herself?"

Shane thought for a while and sipped his tea. He could, by no manner of reasoning, figure out where Theresa might be.

"Maybe somebody died," Jim said, "At Barrière Lake or somewhere, and she just jumped on a bus."

"If she had taken a bus, she would have called me at the first stop," Shane said.

Shane thought for a while. Then he said, "There's a woman at the Indian Affairs office in Montreal named Agatha. Theresa used to have lunch with her once in a while."

"Call her," said Jim, then he waited expectantly while Shane got various operators and receptionists and finally got through to Agatha.

Jim watched Shane's face. He spoke to the woman for a moment and was polite and then very hopeful. It appeared that Agatha knew where Theresa was. Jim sat up attentively. And then he heard his friend blurt out, "She what!", say a few words of thanks and put down the telephone receiver gently.

"Well?" Jim said.

Shane poured a cup of tea and sat back on the living room sofa. The look on his face was a vacant one. "She called

Agatha up around noon. She told her about having passed the entrance examination to the University of Montreal law school because Agatha hadn't heard about it before then. She said that she and Agatha should go out for a beer to celebrate. Agatha said that she had something to do after work that was very important and that she could not go along with Theresa."

"Then what happened?" Jim asked.

"Agatha doesn't really know. She told Theresa she couldn't go, and Theresa just said that it was too bad she couldn't and that was that."

"You think Theresa might have gone out by herself?" Jim asked.

"I'm wondering about that."

"Any idea where?"

Shane hesitated a moment before speaking. "Agatha said that Theresa invited her to a place on Crescent Street where she usually goes."

"What do you mean by 'where she usually goes?'"

"Well, Agatha said that Theresa goes there from time to time to have a beer and a sandwich."

"Anything wrong with that?" Jim asked.

"Geez!" Shane exclaimed, with some impatience, to his friend. "How do you think she lost her two kids? Alcohol. How do you think her father happened to beat her mother and made it so Theresa and her brother and sister had to be given up for adoption? Alcohol. There's no mystery there. Theresa should not drink alcohol any more than her father should have. One lousy beer, one lousy beer can start her drinking again. 'Where she usually goes.' I didn't know about this. It's just a bad, bad situation waiting to happen."

Shane left the apartment and headed downtown in the direction of Crescent Street.

The barmaid was attracted to him; he could tell that. What on other occasions would have been fairly agreeable flattery was now only an annoyance, and he pressed on.

"Did you by chance see an Indian girl…"

"Theresa," the barmaid said.

Shane was surprised that she knew Theresa's name.

"She comes in once in a while for a sandwich and a couple of beers."

Shane shuddered. "Was she in today?"

"She left an hour ago."

"Did she drink anything?" Shane asked, not really wanting to hear the answer.

"Oh, yeah. She had a sandwich and then a couple of beers, and then later she had a few more. She met a couple of guys here. Say, is she a friend of yours or something? Your sister?"

"Yeah," Shane said. "Where did they go?"

"Well," said the barmaid, "they played pool here for a while, and Theresa looked like she was having a good time. They were buying her beer. Then as the afternoon wore on, the three of them said that they were hungry, and that they ought to find some Chinese food. So she left with the two of them, and they said they were going to have something to eat at a Chinese restaurant."

"Do you know which one?" Shane asked.

"No."

"Jim, can you come downtown?" Shane asked his friend over the telephone.

"Sure," Jim said, and he knew how worried his friend was.

Shane gave him the address of a restaurant just off Crescent Street.

II

"So, that's the story," Shane said, after he and Jim had ordered a coffee in the restaurant on Sainte-Catherine.

"Is that bad?" Jim asked.

"It's very bad," Shane said. "One beer leads to two leads to three, and then who knows what can happen," he said worriedly.

"Did the woman in the bar tell you what the two men looked like?"

"She said they were French, both with mustaches and about five feet, eight inches tall."

"That sounds like every second man in the city."

"That is what I thought," said Shane.

They both sat in silence for a while, drinking their coffee.

"How about the Chinese restaurant?" asked Jim hopefully.

"Do you know how many of them there are in Montreal?" Shane said.

"Well," Jim said, "why not start with the ones in the downtown area? If they want to go to a Chinese restaurant, they aren't going to go all the way out to Snowdon."

"You're probably right," Shane said. Why don't you go south of Sainte-Catherine? I'll go north and we'll both head east, and in a couple of hours take the bus back to the restaurant here."

Shane had taken out the telephone directory and quickly listed all the Chinese restaurants north of Sainte-Catherine. He started off on de Maisonneuve, where most of them were located, and occasionally went north or south of the street to find those that were off the main avenue.

The Chinese restaurants began to look all the same to him. The decor of some was plainer than the decor of others, another difference was the degree to which the people in charge spoke English. "Indian woman" didn't register with some of them, and when they seemed to understand the phrase, Shane wondered whether they did not understand it to mean Indian from India.

Longing to catch sight of Theresa, no matter what the circumstances, he did not find her in any of the restaurants. He tried to determine in his own mind what he would do if he found her in one of the Chinese restaurants. Would he become very angry at the men, or at Theresa, or both? He knew he would not. He would be so happy at seeing Theresa that he would take her home to warmth and safety. He would give thanks that she was safe, and he would accept the situation. It was the Indian way.

But he did not find Theresa, and again he thought of all the things that could have happened to her. The fact that she had left the bar with the two men was not good. Could they have hurt her? Even if they had had supper with her at a Chinese restaurant and gone away on their own, Theresa did not belong outside of her apartment when she had been drinking. Anything could befall her.

On the east part of Montreal, well outside of the business district, Shane took a bus and rode it back to the centre for his rendezvous with Jim.

Jim was not at the restaurant when he arrived. Shane ordered a coffee, though he knew it to be the wrong thing for his nervous stomach. Now that he thought of it, the search and the worry were starting to affect him physically. His face, which some had said did not smile enough, was now screwed up into the most worrisome frown, the facial muscles tightening so

much that he now had a headache. What had started as a nervous stomach earlier in the afternoon was now becoming something intolerable.

He looked around the restaurant many times for Jim, but
he did not see him. He looked out the window to see if his
friend was coming up the street or stepping off the bus.
Finally, to see if he could calm himself down, he went to the
pay telephone in the entry. He called Victoria, Mrs. MacNeil,
and his own apartment (to see if by chance someone would
answer), and even tried, rather unreasonably, the law school
and Agatha at Indian Affairs. No one had heard from
Theresa.

He went to the booth, sat down, and accepted when the
waitress offered another cup of coffee.

When in the hell was Jim going to get back? he asked himself. Maybe Jim had some sort of lead that would have taken
him off in another direction. It was true that they had no
way to contact each other, save for meeting again in the restaurant. He could just visualize having to leave the restaurant
and look for Jim. He didn't like the idea at all.

Just as Shane was about to leave the restaurant, he saw Jim
coming through the door. He sat up in anticipation.

"Did you find her?" Shane asked.

"Yes," Jim said.

Shane's spirits soared." Where?"

"A Chinese restaurant about six blocks down on Boulevard
René-Lévesque."

"You don't look very happy about it," Shane observed.

"I missed her by an hour," Jim said dejectedly. "She was
with the two men and they left."

"Was she drinking?"

"Yes."

They were both silent for a while and avoided looking at each other.

Finally Jim spoke, "What do you want me to do, Shane?"

"I don't know," he said as he gave out a deep sigh. "I don't know. Maybe they went from the restaurant to a bar."

"There are lots of bars in downtown Montreal," Jim pointed out.

"I know. But it's either that or they took her some place and did something to her."

"Don't get upset if we don't know anything yet," Jim urged his friend. "We've got nothing else to do that will help, so why don't we both walk the streets on the chance we'll see her. You go in one direction and I'll go in the other. We can ask people we see if they've seen her. There aren't that many Indian women in Montreal."

"That might be the best thing," Shane said. "But first I'm going to call the hospital emergency rooms and the police. It will at least ease my mind. I'll see you back in the apartment later on."

III

Shane walked the streets. He felt very lonely. He imagined his life without Theresa, and he could not do so. He checked in various bars and with some people on the street, and no one had seen a young Indian woman. He was sorry that he had not asked Jim to come with him; his friend's presence would have eased the loneliness considerably.

Up and down the streets he walked until he was almost in a daze. Scores of thoughts raced through his mind, from the various bad things that could have befallen Theresa to his own mistake in not seeing that they had left Montreal and settled either near Moose Factory or near Barrière Lake. Theresa was obviously vulnerable in an urban environment. He kept blaming himself. He thought about Theresa and the many fine times they had shared together. He thought about how much he loved her. The most mundane experiences from the past, shared with her, now became rich, warm memories. What he wouldn't give to again be able to go and with her get yellow birch for snowshoes and have her make lunch. She enjoyed that much more than going to Place des Arts. He remembered the first time he saw her. It was at the Indian Friendship Centre. He noticed her in a crowd of other Indians. It was her striking smile that made her stand out from the others.

He finally saw two Indian women walking along de Maisonneuve. He walked up to them quickly but neither was Theresa. He spoke to them but neither knew Theresa, nor had they seen an Indian woman fitting her description.

On he walked. He felt as though he was going to be driven crazy with his thoughts. If Theresa were in trouble he knew that she would be thinking of him and hoping that he would come to rescue her. It occurred to him that, in the midst of any trouble, she would also be worrying about her kitten, Annie.

Foot-weary, Shane entered his apartment near midnight. Jim was sitting at the kitchen table reading the paper and drinking tea.

"Anything?" Shane said.

"No. How about you?"

"No," said Shane, as he took a deep breath.

Jim looked at his friend. Poor Shane, the handsome young man who people always said did not smile enough — he and Theresa were striking opposites in that respect — now looked as though depression was chiselled into his face. He had never seen him so and could not have imagined any human looking so lost and helpless.

"Some tea?" Jim asked.

"Yes, thanks," Shane said. "I'm going to make some more telephone calls. It's midnight but I have to."

He again called the police, the hospital emergency rooms, Victoria, Mrs. MacNeil and anyone else he could think of. No one had any news of Theresa.

"Get some sleep," suggested Jim. "There's nothing you can do tonight."

Shane tossed in bed for hours without sleeping. Jim slept, but from time to time he would wake up and realize that his friend was not yet sleeping. The crazy thoughts which had tortured Shane earlier, about what possibly might have happened to Theresa, now came back to him in the loneliness of the night. They seemed all the more horrible and tormented him viciously.

Theresa had changed his life. Neither his fine snowshoe craftsmanship, nor success in hunting, nor work with his people would give him the fulfillment he found in her.

He rose and left the apartment and walked the streets for a couple of hours, hoping that it would help him sleep upon his return. But he spent the remainder of the night staring into the darkness.

IV

At seven o'clock, Jim rose and made a big breakfast of eggs, home fries, toast, and coffee.

"Have something to eat," he said to Shane. "I made everything you like."

Shane poured some coffee, remained essentially speechless and was unable to eat anything. He got up and called Victoria, Mrs. MacNeil, the hospitals and the police; no one had any news of Theresa. He came back, stood at the back of his chair and announced to Jim, "I'm going out."

"Where?"

"I'm going back to that Chinese restaurant where they last saw her. I'm going to wander around that area for a while. It's the only thing I can think of to do right now."

He wandered around the area of the Chinese restaurant for a couple of hours then went into a phone booth to ring Theresa's apartment to ask Victoria if she had heard anything from Theresa.

When the telephone was picked up on the other end, all Shane could hear was crying.

"Theresa! I'll be right there!"

He dropped the receiver, ran out of the telephone booth and, for the first time in his life, took a taxi.

He leapt up the stairs to Theresa's apartment. He opened the door. She was standing before him, crying uncontrollably. Her face, neck and arms had been bruised. She ran to him, crying, and as soon as she was safe in his arms, he too began to weep.

He held her for a long time, until her crying subsided. Then he asked her, "Do you want to go to the hospital?"

She nodded that she did.

Chapter Fifteen

I

In the next days they went to the bush as often as they could. Shane was gratified and amazed at Theresa's recuperative powers. She always had liked to be in the woods best. When she was there with Shane and her little kitten, she was content, what had gone on before mattered little.

"Are you getting excited about law school?" Shane asked.

"I definitely am," Theresa said.

They were in a canoe on a small northern pike lake near Saint-Donat. Theresa sat in the bow seat, Shane in the stern, and it was he who paddled to position them for casting. He looked at her often and was gratified to see that she looked happy. She enjoyed fishing, as she never ceased to point out to him when they had a free weekend.

"I'm very happy for you that you were accepted to law school, but a little sad for us," Shane said.

"Are you worried again about being trapped in the city?" she said.

"Yes, more than ever now. It's evil."

"You're right. But if I don't do what I can for Indians, there aren't many people who will."

Shane admired her determination in the face of a challenge that was not going to be easy for her — in more ways than one.

They caught several pike and went home with more than twenty pounds of the succulent fish.

Driving back south along the Autoroute, Shane asked about Victoria.

"Are you going to try to get her another job?"

"I don't know. It's hard for her here. She's lived all her life in Barrière Lake."

"Do you think she should go back?"

"She can't really go back, but it's hard for her to stay too. Montreal isn't a good place for her either."

One Sunday night when they get back to Theresa's apartment in Montreal after a weekend of fishing during which they had slept in a tent, Theresa mentioned off-handedly that she was going to see the doctor the following day.

"Is all the fresh air getting to you?" Shane teased.

She gave him a sidelong glance.

"Pregnant?" he teased. He knew that she wanted very much to have a baby by him but doubted that she wanted it just now, in view of the fact that she was facing three years of law school.

"No. A check-up," she said, to stop his taunting.

"What's wrong?"

"Nothing. It's just that my folks" — she meant the MacNeils — "always had us get a medical check-up once a year. I got used to it because I think it is a good idea."

"Sure, why not," Shane said.

"You should go too, you know. There's nothing wrong with it. You might catch something before it catches you."

"Why worry about it unless something's bothering you?"

"I just want to do it, that's all," said Theresa. "Do you want me to make an appointment with the same doctor for you?"

"No, I'll pass," said Shane.

"I'd like you to go."

"Come on. I don't even get winded when we snowshoe. Gee, you really get spooky sometimes. What do you expect to happen? We're both in our twenties."

"I just think it's a good idea."

Theresa went to the doctor's the next day. Shane stayed home and read.

Theresa came home before six. They sat down to the spaghetti Shane had prepared, just about the only dish he felt confident making. The noodles were floating in liquid, as was the sauce, but Theresa gamely went along with it. Victoria accepted the putative spaghetti as well and said almost nothing during the meal.

"What did the doctor say'?" Shane asked.

"He gave me a check-up and told me to come back to see the results of the tests," Theresa said.

"Pregnant, eh?"

"No, it can't be that."

Thinking that Victoria must get out of Montreal, at least temporarily, they took a long weekend and travelled up to Barrière Lake. Delores had said that it was better for Victoria not to go into the village because of the mysterious thing that had happened, but she could come out to a place out in the woods called Kokomisville — Grandmother City. Here Delores, her sister and their mother had a camp that consisted of several log cabins. They spent the weekend working. Shane cut and split some firewood for the women. All the women, including Victoria, worked at various stages of moose-hide tanning, on the preparation and weaving of a rabbitskin blanket, and netted some fish and then came back to camp to prepare the catch. Mary made bannock and mixed in whole kernel corn. They dunked it in honey and ate it. Most of the meals consisted of generous helpings of moose meat and potatoes.

Victoria spent much of her time beating moose hides with a stick to further the tanning process. It was a job she had done often before and Shane and Theresa were pleased to see Victoria enjoying something at last.

Mary told Shane to fetch a large frying pan from another cabin in the camp.

"My sister-in-law is in the cabin," Mary told Shane. "Just ask her where it's hanging, and tell her I need it."

Shane walked to the other cabin. It was a twelve by sixteen-foot cabin of logs, with a meagre board door. He looked in to see Mary's sister-in-law sitting on the bed nursing a tiny baby. He averted his eyes.

"Could Mary have the frying pan?" he asked.

The sad-faced woman only looked to the frying pan hanging on the wall. Shane took that as permission to borrow it.

He lowered the frying pan from its hook, then started to leave the cabin. He glanced at the infant suckling noisily at the woman's breast. It struck him as strange that the woman did not look especially contented; she looked dejected.

The infant was clothed in a dainty white dress. On its head was a small white cotton bonnet. It had a flap that hung down on the neck to protect the neck from mosquitoes. It was the kind of bonnet found nearly always on the heads of Indian infants in the isolated settlements — and rarely elsewhere.

Shane recoiled as he suddenly realized that it was not an infant at the woman's breast but rather a tiny beaver kit.

When he returned to Mary's cabin with the frying pan, he sat at the kitchen table with Theresa. She offered him a cup of tea that she had just prepared.

Somewhat shaken by what he'd just seen in the other cabin, Shane began, "Your sister-in-law…"

"She lost her baby last week," Mary began in explanation. "I got her a baby beaver to take the place for a while."

Later that afternoon, Mary prepared a large bowl of rice pudding with raisins for all of them for supper.

"*Ki ta madjipiton agwatcing*," Mary said to Victoria, who then set the bowl to cool on the doorstep of the cabin.

They sat there, drinking tea, when all of a sudden, a few minutes later, Shane sprang towards the door quickly, shouting, "Birds!"

And a small, but stealthy, flight of birds had quickly swooped down and picked the rice pudding clean of raisins.

The women had been startled when he had shouted. But when he came back in with the large bowl of rice, now without a raisin in it, and the women saw that the birds had so cleverly robbed them, they howled with laughter and delight — Shane joining them. Perhaps never on the planet had sixteen or seventeen raisins given rise to such amusement.

They left Kokomisville for the long trip back to Montreal gifted with many pounds of maple sugar, moose meat, and fish.

II

Theresa went back to the doctor the next week. Shane was in school. After the appointment, Theresa went to the university where she found Shane in his class. The teacher was in the middle of a lecture, but Theresa managed to get Shane's attention and motion to him to come out of the class.

"Should we take a walk?" she said.

She looked so serious that Shane returned to the class to get his things without even asking what was on her mind.

They walked out of the university building and along the paved paths, beyond the university grounds to the mountain.

They held hands and walked across the green mountain top. Shane still hadn't spoken. He waited for Theresa to say something.

"I'm going to die," she said.

"You're crazy!" Shane shot back. He even started to laugh. But he could see by her seriousness that she was not kidding.

"The doctor told me today when I went back. He got the results from the first tests."

Shane was still unbelieving and hoped that she was kidding. "What is it?"

"Leukemia."

Shane's face was flushed. The announcement caused a reaction that sent shock waves throughout his body. "Is he sure?"

"There's no way he could have made a mistake," she said. Her voice was steady, virtually free from emotion. "It's kind of far along," she said. She was almost apologetic in her tone, as if her illness were her fault.

A score of thoughts crowded Shane's mind instantly, including Theresa's physical condition in recent months. "In the past couple of months you haven't had the strength you usually have."

They continued walking in silence. Neither one had had the time to assess what this would mean to them. Shane looked at Theresa's hopes for the months to come. They were apparently slim. The only thing he could do in the circumstances was to act natural. But how to act natural when one's lover is dying?

That evening after supper Shane went out for a walk by himself to try to think things out. His thoughts were jumbled. Either it would happen or it wouldn't. The only thing he could contemplate clearly was her survival. If she were truly as sick as it appeared, he didn't know what he could do. He couldn't begin to fathom how much he'd miss her.

The next day Shane went in to see the doctor. Dr. James Saarinen was a man in his fifties, very soft-spoken and intelligent. Although still incredulous and shocked at the news, Shane pumped the physician for hard information. He spoke to Shane openly, explaining all the symptoms and realities of Theresa's condition. Most of the information made no sense to Shane, but its effect was only too clear.

The doctor told Shane that Theresa probably had one year to live. She might survive a few months longer at most, but that would require a good deal of luck and care. He would begin treating her immediately. Her first symptoms would be weakness and lethargy, but drugs he would use would mask those problems. They would also stimulate her appetite and give her strength. In fact, with luck and the proper treatment she would be almost symptom-free for many months. Only during the final months would she need hospitalization and then pain could be fought off with drugs. But during the final months, the inevitable onslaught of the leukemia would lay waste to her body. She would be drastically thin and pale.

Shane could hardly visualize Theresa as anything less than smiling and healthy. "It will kill me to see her like that, Doctor," he said.

Chapter Sixteen

I

Jim and Shane were sitting in the kitchen of their apartment having coffee.

"I can't imagine you without her," Jim said.

"I can't either," Shane responded.

Shane looked at his friend and saw in his face a look that might have been there had his friend's entire family been killed in an automobile accident.

"You don't look good," Shane said.

"I put myself in your place."

"Thank you for being so good," Shane said.

"What did the doctor tell you?"

"Basically, he said she could live months or a year and a few months. It's hard for him to say."

"Is there any chance of a remission?" Jim asked.

"There might have been had they found it earlier. Now, it seems to be fairly advanced."

"She's never had a lot of luck, has she?" Jim observed.

"Do you know any Indian who has? Why couldn't this happen to some white man who's been a shyster all his life?"

"What will you do now?"

"I don't really know. It depends on what she wants to do. There's no chance of law school now anyway."

They sat in silence for a time, both fidgeting nervously with their coffee cups.

Shane began again. "There's one thing I can think of to do in the near future — leave Montreal."

Shane and Theresa were sitting in the living room of her apartment, playing chess. It was the week after they had been told the news of her illness.

"You look so beautiful it's hard to imagine you sick," Shane said.

Her face was tanned so that her Indian visage was even darker. She had just washed her hair and it hung down straight and shiny over the chessboard. They each had a cup of hot tea.

Shane found it difficult to believe that Theresa was going to die. There was no logic to it. But he tried to keep himself from displaying his sorrow in front of her.

Their daily lives had not changed; she still went to classes at the university every morning. The only variation in their daily routine was Theresa's frequent visits to the doctor. She would need something to occupy her time and her mind until the end. They would go hiking and canoeing soon, while she still had the strength.

II

Shane was helping Jim make the cross pieces for a pair of Cree snowshoes. "You're going to have to fill some of the orders for snowshoes," he said to his friend as Jim worked away with the crooked knife in the living room.

"You're preoccupied," Jim pointed out.

"You can say that again," Shane said.

"Wouldn't it be good if you worked hard making snow-shoes? It might take your mind off Theresa's illness."

"I can't think of anything else. If anything could divert my mind, snowshoes would be it. But there is no way I can focus my thoughts on anything but her."

"What are you going to do?" Jim asked.

"I'd like to find something that would take her mind off her sickness, but I can't think of what that would be."

"Do you think she is depressed?"

Shane thought a moment. "She doesn't appear to be. She spends a lot of time trying to cheer me up, and seems contented enough given her circumstances. But there's really no way to tell how she is really feeling. You know how she laughs at every chance, and how she's always smiling."

"You think she's covering up her feelings?" Jim asked.

"Yes. She has to be thinking about her illness a great part of the time. But it's impossible to tell. I know that she worries about what's going to happen to me afterwards. Obviously she puts on a happy face to lift my spirits."

Jim took a look at Shane and said wryly, "She's not really succeeding."

Shane parked his truck in front of Theresa's apartment. He thought he would surprise Theresa and take her out to a movie and dinner. He hadn't even called to announce he was coming over. A smile lit his face when he thought of the pleasure he gave to Theresa when he gave her a gift or surprised her with some special kind of attention. He took a bouquet of flowers from the front seat of the truck and hurried through the door of the apartment building. He mounted the stairs two at a time until he was on Theresa's floor. He smiled in delight at how much she was going to enjoy the surprise. He went down the mail corridor and then turned to the little side corridor where Theresa's door was located.

As he turned the corner, he reeled in shock. There was blood coming out from under her door.

He dropped the bouquet and ran to the door, "Theresa! Theresa!" he shouted as he furiously attempted to open the door.

At last, unable to get the door open, he backed up and madly kicked the door several times until it gave way.

There was a body lying face down in a pool of blood on the floor of the kitchen. "Theresa!" he shouted again. Then as he bent down he saw that it was not Theresa but rather Victoria. "Oh, God," he exclaimed.

She had slit her wrists.

He bent down to check her. He was sure she was dead. Then he called the ambulance. As he looked at the body in horror, an insane thought came to him: how beautiful was her lustrous black hair against the bright red blood.

Shane and Theresa called the Barrière Lake band office to let Delores know what had happened. They arranged for the body to be sent back to Barrière Lake to be buried at the old Indian cemetery. Shane was surprised to see that the shock of Victoria's death had for a time seemed to push thoughts of Theresa's illness from their minds. They talked about Victoria and what a short and tragic life she had had.

One evening they were playing chess in her apartment.

"Well," Theresa said, "it looks like you'll have to get someone else to help you have that baby we talked about having."

Shane winced very slightly. Although she had said it without any emotion, he knew she must be hurting inside.

"Of course it's a good way to get zero population growth," she said, "have the mother die."

Shane motioned for her to move her piece, hoping to distract her.

"And what about taking to the bush?" she said. "Remember how we talked about hunting and raising our food and building a log cabin? You'll have to do it by yourself now."

"Don't say that," Shane said. "If we talk only about what might have been, we'll both go crazy."

Theresa got pensive. Her mind was no longer on the chess game. She stared at the pieces but concentrated on something else. Finally, a broad smile spread across her face.

"Shane?" she said, drawing the name out slowly.

"Yeah?"

"Let's do what we planned to do."

"Do what?"

"Everything we wanted to do," she said, her eyes lighting up and her smile almost boundless. "Let us move to the bush and have a baby."

"Oh, Theresa," Shane said very sadly. Hearing her long after fantasies that would never be realized almost made him weep.

"No, Shane, listen," she went on. "We can do it." She was excited now. "It's only the end of May. We can do it. We'll have the baby and move to the bush."

Shane's eyebrows rose in disbelief.

"There's enough time for a baby," she insisted. "We'll just move it up a little in our plans."

Shane was silent, thinking about the idea. Then he spoke. "I told Jim I thought we'd probably move out of Montreal soon."

"We'll build a cabin in the bush. Do you remember what we talked about? We said we'd go to some lake deep in the bush and build a cabin."

Shane thought about it for a moment. "Do you think there is enough time?'"

"Maybe yes, maybe no," she said. "We don't know for sure. But I know that there isn't anything I'd rather be doing with that time than trying."

He was now taken with her passion and every modification of it. Not only could he see that these crazy plans would be marvellous for her, but they were already making him come alive. He had forgotten how alive he could feel. Not in a long time had he felt so free.

They found a large map of Quebec and spread it out. There were lakes everywhere. Untouched lakes. Tens of thousands of them. More lakes than there were in all of the United States.

After studying the map for a short while, Theresa said, "Let's go here." She put her finger on the map and held it there until Shane could pick it out.

"Lac des Îles — Lake of the Islands," she said. "It's right near this little village, Casey. There's a Canadian National track going through it." Theresa was happy with her choice. She said the name of the lake over and over again, as if the sound of it would give a clue as to what it would be like.

Shane called the Canadian National station the next day. There was a daily passenger service going through Casey. He found out that not only did the train stop at Casey but because it was a wilderness service, it stopped wherever along the line the passenger wanted to get off. The woman in the information office told him that the only thing he had to do was tell the conductor where he wanted to stop. To catch the train again at the same point, he simply had to flag it down.

Chapter Seventeen

I

"But she will be away from medical care," Dr. Saarinen said when Shane went to see him at Montreal General Hospital.

"If she has to die, she really wants to die in the bush," said Shane, sitting in a chair in front of the doctor's desk.

"Well," said the doctor, trying to understand, "I guess I would too. But at the same time, I think I'd want the best medical care possible to prolong life as much as possible."

"I think Theresa feels that a shorter life in the bush is better than life prolonged in Montreal."

Dr. Saarinen said, "She's Indian. I can understand that."

"Are you sure it's terminal?" Shane asked with a glimmer of hope in his voice.

"I would say so. It's an advanced case. The chances of a remission always exist, of course, but they are exceedingly slim."

"Couldn't I administer some of the medicine to her?" Shane asked.

"Some, I guess."

"Then that would allow us to go in the bush," Shane said.

"To some extent," Dr. Saarinen agreed.

They looked at each other, her physician and her husband, feeling helpless.

"I'll tell you what we can do," Dr. Saarinen said. "I'll give you some literature on the drugs now, and you can come back with Theresa in a few days. Then the three of us together can discuss whether some kind of medical treatment in the bush would he feasible."

Shane asked hopefully, "Couldn't just being in the bush help psychologically — and physically?"

"I don't discount that."

"There's another thing, Doctor. Theresa and I always thought that we would have a child."

"I'm sorry."

"Well," Shane began, hoping that he would be able to elicit some enthusiasm, "we'd like to try now."

"It would be very difficult, given the time frame you have," Dr. Saarinen said.

"It's very important to me and to her. When she's no longer around, I want to have someone who is part of us. And Theresa wants to leave something that's a part of us."

"I can understand that," Dr. Saarinen said. "In a way, though, it would be a medical burden upon her. Her body would be trying to fight this disease — not to mention the drugs — while trying to nourish the baby. You would be limiting the range of drugs that could be used; also, some of the drugs are very powerful, and they are potential mutagens."

"And if she got pregnant, the baby could be a psychological help and give her something to live for — for a while at least. And that could help her physically."

Dr. Saarinen said, smiling, "You may be right."

"Well?"

"It's possible," the physician said, "if she conceived right away. But I wouldn't recommend it. You see, in her last weeks, she isn't going to have much strength. It would be a question of seeing whether she would die before coming to term. It would actually be a toss-up. And you certainly wouldn't want to risk the baby's life."

"But we want the baby, Doctor — badly."

"I certainly wouldn't stop you even if I could," the doctor said. "She doesn't have much time left. She might as well spend her last days the way she wants to, even if it costs her a few months."

"Thank you, Doctor."

"There's one more thing."

"Yes?"

"If you do it this way, you'll have to think about the possibility of complications during birth. You'll be in the bush, after all. If a breech birth happens, you'll need some sort of preparation. But we'll attend to that later."

They both stood up. Dr. Saarinen came around the front of his desk to shake Shane's hand.

"Thank you, Doctor," Shane said, then turned to leave.

Dr. Saarinen put his hand on Shane's shoulder. "Shane, I admire you and Theresa for this."

II

Dr. Saarinen fixed an appointment for Shane and Theresa with a gynaecologist.

"If we have a baby, you're going to have to be the midwife," Theresa said.

"I've been thinking about that," Shane said. "If you can handle your part, I'll handle mine."

They went to see the gynaecologist with Dr. Saarinen's referral stating that, as far as he could see, she could have a baby. The gynaecologist concurred, although he was also reticent about having it far from professional care. Still, he was helped along by Dr. Saarinen who was by now sympathetic to their plans, even if they were incompatible with sound medical practice.

The gynaecologist did the same thing for Shane that Dr. Saarinen had done; he gave him some books to read about childbirth. Then he brought him back later to witness a live birth, with the mother's permission. He showed Shane, step by step, how to deliver a baby. Shane found the whole procedure rather uncomplicated — until the gynaecologist began talking about haemorrhages. They both dreaded the possibility of having any complications in the bush. But the doctor told Shane that a normal delivery — assuming Theresa's strength held up — would be relatively easy. If the odds held, they wouldn't have any problems.

Shane visited Dr. Saarinen again and told him all the things that the gynaecologist had asked him to study.

"It sounds as though he gave you a very good short course," Dr. Saarinen said. "Did he tell you about a Caesarean section?"

"No," Shane said.

"He probably didn't think it would happen or that if it did, you should not attempt to do anything about it. Caesarean sections are done in cases of breech births or in instances of cross births, where the long axis of the child lies across the long axis of the mother. Those kinds of births are actually rather rare, but it's something we need to think about. By the way, have you ever seen animals give birth?"

"Yes," said Shane, "often."

"Have you ever butchered a large animal?"

"Many."

"Well," said Dr. Saarinen, "we can plan for this unlikely eventuality, but don't tell the medical board I'm showing you these things or I'll have to take to the bush myself. Theresa has delivered vaginally twice before so it is unlikely she would have to deliver abdominally. But if she does, I want you to cut the baby out."

Shane's eyebrows rose.

"The reasons why are obvious," the doctor went on. "She will be near death from leukemia. In our hypothetical situation — which, I emphasize, is extremely unlikely — she would be facing almost certain death, which would therefore indicate a Caesarean section. I hope you have a sharp knife."

"I test it by shaving the hair on my arm."

Dr. Saarinen smiled. "I'll show you what to look for, how to make the incisions in the abdominal wall and the uterus and then how to take the baby and suture the uterus and the abdominal wall. In the nineteenth century, a Caesarean section nearly always resulted in the death of the mother from sepsis or haemorrhage — or they had to cut the baby's head. But I think with some intelligent instructions and some antiseptic procedures, you could do a better job than a physician could have in the nineteenth century. In any case, saving the baby would be better than losing them both."

"Do you know," Theresa said to Shane later, when he had explained the medical situation to her, "it's kind of a strange situation. If I have complications, I bleed to death. If I don't have complications, I die anyway."

Chapter Eighteen

I

"We'll need a canoe," Theresa pointed out.

"We have a canoe."

"No, I mean a real canoe," she said.

"A birch-bark canoe? The people at Moose Factory haven't made birch-bark canoes for decades, maybe since the turn of the century. I don't know if anyone there would be capable of making a canoe anymore."

"Delores told me once that there is an old man out in the bush at Barrière Lake who can still make them."

"How will I learn before we go to Lac des Îles?" Shane asked.

"How long do you think it takes to make one?" Theresa answered with a question of her own.

"Maybe two or three weeks. But you know, they aren't really easy things to make; it's quite a sophisticated craft."

"Many people say you make the best snowshoes they have ever seen."

"That's not the same thing as a birch-bark canoe. It's much harder to get the materials and the work itself is different."

"But you're very skilled. You can do it."

"Maybe," Shane said. "If there were time."

Theresa managed to reach Delores through the band office, though it took some doing before someone was able to locate her.

"The old man," Delores said after Theresa explained that Shane wondered if it would be possible to come north to Barrière Lake to learn how to make a birch-bark canoe, and if there would be a builder who might be willing to teach him. "Patrick Matchewan. His camp is about thirty miles in the bush. He's a very good canoe builder, and he makes snow-shoes and *tikinagans* too."

Shane was listening in the kitchen and could make out what was being said at the other end of the telephone connection.

He motioned to Theresa to put her hand over the receiver. "We don't really have much time," he said. "Why don't you see if Delores would hire a driver today and go out to see him and ask him if I can come up there to make a canoe with him? Maybe if Delores told him the circumstances that would help. Then she could call back here collect."

Delores called back that evening. Patrick Matchewan would gladly take on an apprentice, and Shane could come any time.

"I'd better go tomorrow, then," Shane said. "Dr. Saarinen said he wants to have you in for some treatments. Maybe you can get some of our things ready while I'm at Barrière Lake."

II

Shane started before dawn the next morning and reached Barrière settlement by late morning. Delores drew him a crude map of the thirty-mile bush trip back to Patrick Matchewan's cabin.

The entire trip from the Barrière village was over wilderness gravel roads, now mercifully dry after the spring thaw. Shane drove on one of the little bush tracks that went off to the side and came upon a lake one-fourth of a mile across. It was surrounded by black spruce. There was a clearing at the end of the little dirt track.

Shane was heartened when he saw smoke coming from the chimney of a little log cabin built in the quickly erected, *pièce-en-pièce* style, of the kind Shane himself had often helped build in the woods at Moose Factory.

Shane went up to the door and opened it slowly. Patrick Matchewan was sitting inside on a straight-backed chair puffing away slowly on his pipe. He had hair flecked with gray that fell to his shoulders. Shane could see the effect of decades of sunlight and winter cold on his skin. He wore old boots, and his long-sleeved shirt was buttoned right up to the neck.

The man nodded to Shane that he should come in.

Shane was at first reluctant to speak, fearing that his less-than-perfect Algonquin would be a little difficult for Patrick Matchewan. He quickly discovered, much to his surprise, that the old man spoke fluent English and French, in addition to his native language.

"Thank you for letting me come here to work with you," Shane said.

Patrick nodded. "Want a tea?" he asked. To Shane's affirmative answer, the old man moved the water kettle on the woodstove from the place where it was being kept warm to the hot spot on the surface, so it would boil again.

As they drank the tea, Shane inquired about the canoe they were to build. "I don't mean to hurry you up or anything," he said apologetically.

"I have the materials for a canoe; I was going to start next week. Tomorrow is as good a time as any," he said, smiling in a way that Shane would come to treasure in the short time he was with the old man. "It's good to have help."

They began work the next morning. Patrick noticed very appreciatively that Shane could easily handle the splitting of the cedar and the carving of the ribs with a crooked knife. Shane was good with a crooked knife, and there was no better way to please an Indian craftsman.

They sat in the shade under two tall black spruce trees, their lower branches cut off. "This is where we have the building bed," Patrick said, "You should keep the hot sun off the bark while the canoe is being made."

And a while later: "We make all the wood for the canoe first, then we put everything together. If you don't have a little system, you don't work well."

Patrick showed Shane how to split the cedar for the ribs. "This is easier to split than ash for snowshoes," Shane observed.

Then they split the very thin sheathing that would be used to line the inner hull of the canoe. Shane and Patrick both sat on large blocks of wood as they finished shaping the ribs and sheathing with their crooked knives. When they finished the ribs and sheathing, they split the long battens that would be the gunwales. From a knot-free cedar log fifteen feet long, they split in halves, quarters, and then again twice, until the battens were nearly the proper dimensions. Then they carved a lissome finish on the gunwales with their crooked knives.

Patrick asked Shane to go in the woods to find a medium-sized yellow birch for the five thwarts. He didn't have to tell the young man from Moose Factory how to split the log and then carve the pieces. For the actual shape of the thwarts,

Patrick simply pointed to his own birch-bark canoe lying nearby. "Just make the thwarts the same way," Patrick said, and he watched Shane with satisfaction while he smoked his pipe.

Talk during the canoe building was almost non-existent. But during breaks when they went in the cabin and made a tea, they spoke of various things. Shane enjoyed talking with Patrick for the same reason he liked speaking to the old people at Moose Factory — they knew so much more than he did. This was especially true about their knowledge of the animals. The old people had more time, and more favourable circumstances, in which to observe the animals and think about them.

Patrick said, "The moose does not die. And the deer and the beaver do not die. They live. Their meat lives in men. Their skins clothe men."

Shane nodded at this observation, something about which he had never thought.

Trapping had changed, the old man said, among the white trappers and the younger Indians. "The beaver, the lynx, and the muskrat are all good to eat. Today the trappers leave the beaver meat and sell the hide to buy bacon. That is not a good thing."

Shane enjoyed the breaks as much as the canoe building and hoped that Patrick would speak on.

Patrick described an involved ritual that was to be followed when a beaver was killed. The head, paws, entrails, and tail all had to be placed in a prescribed pattern. This had to be done with care.

"Why do the Indians do that for a beaver?" Shane asked.

"We must respect them," replied Patrick. "They are so much like Indians. The old people thought that animals were much like Indians, only each possesses attributes the other does not."

Volunteering information was not the Indian way. But Patrick seemed rather firm in his beliefs, even though they were expressed almost diffidently.

Patrick said once, "They say that the Algonquin came from the east."

"Where?" Shane asked.

"East," was the extent of Patrick's reply.

Shane handed a teacup to Patrick, then lifted his own to his lips and sipped quietly before resuming work with the crooked knife. A whiskey-jack swooped close to see if Shane might not be having a morsel of food with his tea. "I wonder where the language came from?" Shane asked.

"It might be that the language came about because the people long ago at first tried to imitate the animal sounds."

III

Something that Shane felt rather than verbalized: in the woods with Patrick there was peace. Not the televisions, radios, and four-wheelers that sometimes smothered his mother's house in Moose Factory. Or the sounds of the city. Even at night in Montreal when nearly everyone was asleep, there was the distant motorized hum of the traffic on the autoroute.

Here, as he drew the crooked knife towards him rhythmically, slowly, and efficiently, leaving the fragrant cedar shavings beneath him, he heard the several voices of the wind, though he almost laughed at how inferior his perception was to that of the old people like Patrick.

But even in his undeveloped stage, Shane could hear what the wind wanted to tell him. As he carved, he could hear in various directions the open, free sound that the wind made as it coursed through a tall white pine; the steady, workaday blowing when it ran through white spruce and black spruce; the sound, close to a tintinnabulation, that it made when it blew through a little stand of poplar to the south — poplar, whose leaves were so lightly attached to their stems that the delicate fluttering they made could only be made by the leaves of this tree; the crackling made by the dead leaves of the maple just behind Patrick's cabin that had died the year before; the lapping of the waves on the shore near them: the wind was so precise about the waves that it told him exactly how high they were and how a canoe would react to them.

IV

In the canoe building, Patrick's movements were deliberate and almost seemed slow at times, but Shane was pleased at how quickly they seemed to be making progress. Patrick had already gathered the single large sheet of bark that would he used to make the canoe. Likewise, his son had helped him gather the cedar for the ribs and sheathing and the spruce root for the lashing.

Patrick's crooked-knife work was methodical and precise. With Shane working alongside, they produced piles of shavings until they almost buried themselves.

Patrick said, "The old people had one name for shavings from a crooked knife. They call them *piwipodjigan*. But they had a different name for shavings from an ordinary knife or a plane or something like that!

Shane knew no equivalent in Cree, and he never ceased to delight in the complexities of the Indian language.

They prepared hundreds of feet of spruce root together, splitting the root first in half and then boiling the root to help remove the bark. The roots would be the lashing for the gunwales.

The large birch-bark sheet was rolled out on the building bed. Patrick instructed Shane to put the building frame on the bark and then to weight it down with hundreds of pounds of stones. They pried up the sides of the bark sheet with birch pickets, then tied the pickets at the tops across the canoe.

Patrick took innumerable eye measurements, making sure the bows lined up perfectly, ascertaining that the inwale frame was the proper height above the bark sheet, making sure that the outwales were fixed at the exact height of the inwales so that they could be lashed together.

Shane, in his enthusiasm, did most of the lashing of the gunwales. He punched holes in the thick bark sheet under the gunwales with the awl. Then he made ten turns around the gunwales with the spruce root.

Patrick showed Shane how to bend the ribs and place them in the canoe for drying. The ribs had been soaking in bunches for several days. When the day came to bend the ribs, Patrick held a pair of ribs over a kettle and boiling water was ladled over them. Patrick took the two ribs and sat down on a log block, then he carefully bent the ribs over his knee in near-perfect conformation with the hull shape. He then took the ribs to the canoe and fitted them snugly against the bottom to dry.

After the ribs had dried in the sun for an entire day, they were removed from the canoe, and Shane helped Patrick to fit the beautiful pieces of cedar sheathing along the entire interior of the canoe. The ribs' ends were pried under the gunwales and the ribs pounded tightly in the canoe to hold the sheathing in place. When the canoe was finished, Patrick showed Shane how to seal the seams of the canoe with spruce gum. The gum was actually a mixture of spruce sap and bear grease, the latter to keep the gum from cracking too easily.

Patrick and Shane paddled the finished canoe around the little lake when it was finished. Shane was honoured to be paddling in the bow of the canoe of a master Indian canoe maker.

Patrick told Shane how they had lived in the woods as children, how none of the family knew a word of any language other than Algonquin. He told stories of hunting in the fall and trapping in the winter, and how they went to the sugar bush in the spring for maple sugar, and how following the seasons in the forest led them also to the blueberry fields in August.

The old man said that the culture was dying. He didn't know as much as his mother and father had known about Indian life; his son and daughter-in-law knew less and his grandchildren much less yet about the Indian way of life. They barely knew the language. They didn't know the woods. They were almost afraid of the woods — like white men were.

"We weren't afraid of the woods," Patrick said as he drew on his pipe. He was sitting on the stump he used for a seat while carving ribs, and had laid down his crooked knife. White people say that the bush is wild. I never thought that the lakes and the hills and the deep forest were wild. They were home. When we came out in the spring to sell the furs at the Hudson's Bay post, it felt as if we were in a different world. But when we turned around and returned into the deep bush far away from the post, it felt almost as if we were in a different world. We didn't think there were wild animals in the bush; they were the animals we lived with. Animals like us.

"Many things were part of our life long ago that aren't part of our life today. We thought about things in a different way than we think about them today."

Listening to Patrick, Shane realized how Indians like himself and Theresa and Delores and Maurice Papati were distant from the kind of life the old people had.

Patrick went on: "When we were in the bush, children were taught to sit still and to enjoy it. They were taught to smell everything, to see what the wind could tell. Their mothers taught them to look when there didn't seem to be anything to see and to listen closely when everything was quiet. A child who cannot remain still is not fully a child."

"Have you ever gone to school?" Shane asked.

"Once. Not long. One season only," Patrick said. "My father was told to send me there by a missionary, although he did not want to. It was not good. It didn't teach Indian things. The Indian children go to white school today, and they are no more Indian. My father took me out right away because he wanted me to go hunting with him. That was better, and I never went back to school. With him I learned the Indian way.

"I could see what they were doing in school. They learned to think with their heads, not with their hearts. Indians start to believe the same way. But they miss things. They don't see things. The spirit cannot talk to reason.

"I tried never to become caught up in the white man's way after that. White men were so busy that they had no time to think and to see. I never worked all the time. When you work, you cannot dream. Wisdom comes in dreams."

Chapter Nineteen

I

"I'm pregnant," Theresa said when Shane walked through the door of their apartment. Her smile beamed from her face, and her eyes closed into slits. Shane thought that her beautiful Indian eyes were a true gift of the race.

"That was quick!" he said, and he ran to hug her and lifted her from the floor. For her to have such a moment of deep happiness was a precious thing to him.

She made tea for them and told Shane what the obstetrician had told her: about her likely due date and how to care for herself during her pregnancy. "What if it's twins?" she asked.

Theresa was unusually voluble and spoke on about the pregnancy as if it were a living child. "We have to take good care of it; we have to feed it well so it will grow. I'll try to keep it warm and comfortable." And she smiled broadly, happy with herself, happy with Shane, and quite delighted at the pregnancy.

Theresa was eager to learn about Patrick Matchewan, what kind of man he was, where he and Shane worked, and how Shane had learned about birch-bark canoe building. Over hours of tea drinking, they spoke about Shane's experiences, the baby, and the move to the bush.

"She's amazing," Shane said to Jim in the apartment they shared, "She's really hard to believe."

"What do you mean?" Jim asked.

"She's got incredible resilience."

"You mean being reasonably cheerful in the face of her illness?"

"Yes. I can't imagine that. Losing her two children, being brought up in a home away from her brothers and sisters and parents, then diagnosed with a terminal illness — and then being able to smile. And they say I don't smile enough in the normal course of things." Shane even then attempted a smile, which made Jim smile at him.

"How do you think she manages that?" Jim asked.

"Well, of necessity maybe. Maybe it's built into the race. Maybe because she's Indian."

II

They made preparations to go north to Lac des Îles. They bought seed for the garden they hoped to have, and Shane bought a bucksaw as he thought it would require less maintenance — and gas — than a chainsaw. He would not have to do a great amount of cutting for a small log cabin and a supply of firewood. He bought a small, old, cast-iron stove. From a demolition site in the city, he bought a window and door frames and some of the other things that he could not easily fashion in the woods.

They accumulated large sacks of flour, salt, sugar, beans, peas, and metal containers of salt pork and lard. Shane and Theresa were so occupied with preparations for the trip that her illness ceased to be their main topic of conversation.

"Will you miss the city?'" Theresa asked.

"No," Shane said. "We've had good times here, though. We met here. We've had certain opportunities here. But this is not home for either of us, and it won't be hard to leave."

Finally they were ready to leave. One day, Jim brought Shane's pick-up truck over to Theresa's apartment in the afternoon. There were so many supplies — which included Shane's canoe — that they had to make two trips to the baggage office of the Canadian National station in downtown Montreal. The train departed every evening at 8 p.m.

They were ready to leave.

The train pulled slowly through the station and through Place Bonaventure. As the train came out at last into the open, Shane and Theresa looked at the city. It stood in the dark against the backdrop of Mount Royal. The searchlight atop the high, cruciform Place Ville Marie panned the city. It would be the last time they would see the city for a long time.

Shane wondered to himself if he had done the right thing, whether it would not actually be better to stay in the city. Theresa would be more comfortable medically and physically. The better care might secure for her an extra few months. But it was Theresa herself who had chosen a better way of living, rather than a longer way.

"Excited?" she asked, holding on to his arm as they watched the lights of Montreal recede into the distance.

"Yes," he said, a little awed at what they were undertaking.

They both took out books to read. Their car was barely a third full. Most of the people were going home to Trois-Rivières or Quebec City from Montreal. Shane and Theresa sat in a double seat facing their own, so they were able to put their feet up and later could stretch out to the other seat to sleep.

Sometime during the middle of the night, they were awakened when the train was jostled.

"We must be in La Tuque," Shane said, "They're changing the cars for the trip to Senneterre."

They could see the lights of the town as they looked, bleary-eyed, out of the window.

In a short time, the train started up again, this time on the trip west that would lead them to Casey.

A conductor came down the aisle to check the tickets. Shane told him where they wanted to get off, at a siding fifteen miles beyond Casey; he showed the man where on the topographical map.

"No problem," said the conductor. "I know the place. We'll be there just after sunrise."

He was a stout man with white hair, just under sixty, Shane guessed.

"What will you be doing there?" he asked.

They told him that they were on their way there to build a cabin and live in the bush.

At this he perked up. They had touched a responsive chord. The conductor was keenly interested in how they planned to do it.

"I have to make the rounds, but do you mind if I come back in a few minutes and talk to you about it?" he asked.

They liked the idea.

He returned a short time later with three large mugs of steaming tea.

"Tell me now," he said. "Will you be making your cabin out of spruce? There's a lot of spruce stands in the area, you know. And what will you be using as chinking?"

Shane answered those questions, and the conductor asked more. He envied them for what they were doing. Each time they answered his questions, he shook his head approvingly, as if they were doing exactly the right thing. He became more and more animated as they told of their plans. He told them that he had once come out here as a trapper, but that he had only lasted a year — until he got married. Then he thought he needed a more steady income. But he had fallen in love with the woods during that winter. He talked of it rapturously — the clear water, the moose he saw nearly every day, the snow so deep in the winter that there were a few times when he couldn't get out of his cabin. He talked on and on, transported by the memory of it all. He brought things to memory that he hadn't thought about for years. And as he told them, he relived the experiences, and he enjoyed them again just as he had years before. There was regret in his voice, as though he thought he might have truly missed something all these years. He had had to work on the railroad to support his family. But he still — passing frequently the territory he had worked as a trapper that brief winter long ago — missed it. Despite the wife and children in La Tuque, in their modern house with electricity, two bathrooms, and television, he missed the wild — and his free life in the wilderness, which he had known for such a short time.

The conductor talked on so long that he went to fill the mugs again with tea.

There was something in him that wasn't satisfied living in a town, something — a longing — whose fulfillment could only have come in the bush.

"I feel it when the train stops at some lonely river to let off a trapper and his supplies, or when an Indian family gets off to canoe back to their camp, or when lumberjacks get off at small villages along the rail line on their way to the lumber camps far back in the bush. I'll never really know what it is like again, to depend on the wilderness to live. The trappings of civilization are too much a part of me."

The conductor then begged Shane and Theresa for more details of their plans. And he listened again as enthusiastically as he had talked of his own dreams.

III

A while later, Shane and Theresa awoke. It was getting light but the sun hadn't yet risen. The train was slowing down for Casey. There was an old building on the south side of the tracks that served as a station and warehouse — mostly warehouse because there wasn't much passenger traffic in the area. Across from that on the north side of the tracks was the little gathering of buildings known as Casey. About fifteen buildings were grouped along the two dirt roads going through the village. The town-site itself was poised between the tracks to the south and the river just to the north.

"Sure you wouldn't like to stay here?" Shane asked Theresa. "All the comforts of home."

"No, let's go on," she laughed, enjoying being teased. "How far is it yet?"

Shane picked up the map and measured off the distance. "Casey's about twelve miles from our stop. Look here. There's an old logging road or something that goes from the tracks up to Lac des Îles. We can carry our things up there if the river from Lac des Îles isn't deep enough for canoeing."

The train left Casey and, as it did, the conductor came to the car to tell them to come back to the baggage car and get ready for their stop.

"You know all these plans of yours about building a cabin," he said slowly and thoughtfully. "Do it. I want to tell you that. Do it. It's a fine idea and don't give it up, I wish I were going along."

The train rolled past a long lake on the south side of the tracks. When it had come nearly to the end of the lake, it slowed and finally stopped.

A trainman opened the door of the boxcar. Shane and Theresa jumped down and then began the long process of taking their things from the boxcar. The trainman and the conductor fed the supplies to the door of the boxcar; Shane and Theresa set them by the side of the tracks. They both struggled with the canoe. When they came to the small wood stove, the trainman jumped down from the boxcar, and the three of them together wrestled the stove to the ground.

They shook hands with the conductor as the train was pulling away, and were left alone in the bright May morning.

Chapter Twenty

I

Shane and Theresa watched the train disappear around the bend. Shane looked at what was going to be their conduit to civilization when they needed it. There were no buildings at the place, just a rundown logging road that, towards the north, would lead them close to Lac des Îles. In either direction along the tracks there would be an early view of the train so that they should have an easy time flagging it down when they needed it. And after the various crews learned that they were in the area, they would keep an eye for them along the tracks.

"There are no flies," said Theresa. "Must be a little early for them here."

"Let's boil the tea pail," she said as she rested for a moment on their dunnage.

Shane emptied an old coffee can of nails and went down to the creek flowing to the lake where he washed the can clean and filled it with water. Hanging from the cooking stick over the fire, it was not long before it was boiling. He threw in some tea bags.

Theresa opened a tin of canned ham and cut slices that she put on their store-bought bread.

After having eaten, they spent an hour moving the supplies into the woods near the tracks. Packing up the canvas wall tent, food and supplies for immediate needs, they started north to Lac des Îles.

The road was a slight one, the remnant of an earlier, small logging operation. Bordered by stands of spruce, with some birch and poplar, its surface was rough and uneven and would have been a difficult passage for a motor vehicle. Smaller vegetation had nearly covered the former roadway. Shane's gaze was on the trail only long enough to keep him from stumbling over something. The rest of the time, he looked all around him on both sides of the road, making an inventory of stands for later use. To the right of the old road was the stream that ran from Lac des Îles in the direction of the tracks. Along the stream, and in a small swamp, were cedars large and small. Beyond the cedars on the far side rose a hardwood hill. "Look at the big birch on the hill," Theresa said. "Maybe there would be one for a canoe there."

"It might take a lot of walking anyway," Shane said.

Their walking was easy; they had only enough supplies to last them a couple of days until they could come back on the first of many return trips they would have to make.

The leaves were just coming out on the trees. Still not completely dry from the spring runoff, the road was muddy and would be hard to negotiate carrying anything heavy.

Over the crest of a small rise, to the right and through a stand of pine, they saw blue water — Lac des Îles, their home and the last one Theresa would know.

Coming up to the lake on its western shore, they stopped a minute to look. It was not a large lake, but it would be big enough for them. It did indeed have some islands — and bays, many little places that would be fun to explore by canoe. The water was still calm; the day's wind had not come up yet.

"Isn't it lovely?" Theresa said to Shane as she walked over to hug him.

"Wait a couple of weeks until the black flies and mosquitoes come out. You'll be ready to go back," he said, knowing she was more likely to put up with it than he was. As long as she still had physical strength, she didn't falter. He marvelled at her energy and endurance; knowing that she was dying yet acting like she had everything to live for. The physical effects of the disease hadn't yet manifested themselves, except for the fatigue that occasionally overtook her. She was as full of life as she had been before, and just as beautiful, Shane thought.

They walked to the shore of the lake and scouted its banks.

"Let's go back and get the canoe," he said. "We aren't going to be able to get through this bush to look for a place to put the tent."

They made the hour's journey back to the tracks. Shane carried the canoe back. Theresa carried more of their dunnage.

They pulled the canoe across the muskeg shore to the lake. Hardly a zephyr broke the surface of the water. They paddled around the shore of the lake from the western side to a small bay in the south. Spruce lined the shore; they knew they had only to find a level spot on the bank, and they would have all the building wood they needed.

Finally they found a place that pleased them — a little indentation of the shoreline that formed a cove. The land sloped gradually down to the lake. On the left, about fifty yards from shore, was a small, tree-covered island. Lac des Îles was only a mile wide: one main body with two large sheltered bays on the east. The cove where they landed faced north.

Within a few hours of coming to the cove, Shane had cut spruce poles. Then he set up the canvas wall-tent. He started to clear some more brush.

"What are you doing?" Theresa asked.

"Cutting this brush. We'll be cutting most of these trees to clear a spot for the cabin. And we've got to get the brush out of the way and burn it.

"Didn't Patrick Matchewan say that when you work, you cannot dream, and that wisdom comes in dreams?"

Shane hesitated, bush in hand.

Theresa said, "If we clear the bush this week or next it doesn't matter. We're here; that's the important thing."

"You're right." He dropped the bush and came over to sit beside her.

The following day they returned to the Canadian National tracks for as much of their belongings as they could carry.

Three days later, there was a large area cleared around the tent site. It wasn't so much that Shane was hungry for work. It was just that he was excited and curious to see what the cabin was going to look like. They had cut birches and some spruce with the saw and then cleared out the underbrush. Theresa worked at digging up sod and roots for a garden.

They slept in the tent, which Theresa had made rather comfortable by laying a bed of spruce boughs on the floor of dirt. The natural cushion also added a nice aroma to the tent but it had to be renewed every two weeks when the needles dried out and the bed lost its springiness.

Every evening, Theresa made a smudge, which she put into the tent before they went to bed. It helped to control the black flies and mosquitoes that had now come out.

During the fly season they did their heaviest work. Theresa had dug and planted the garden. She had to go through the woods to gather usable soil from various spots, which she then transported in a potato bag to the camp. Shane cut spruce trees in the area. Swatting flies created a bloody mess that was mixed with copious sweat and lots of dirt. They sweated doubly because they clothed every square inch of their skin that they possibly could, to ward off flies. They tied their pants tight around the tops of their boots. They wore gloves. Handkerchiefs stuffed under the back of their caps in a kepi-like arrangement kept flies from the neck. The temperature was more than ninety degrees Fahrenheit.

Shane knew his clothes smelled terrible. But there was virtually no other way of warding off flies during the season. He wasn't about to spend the day washing himself and his clothes if an hour later they'd be in the same state.

Theresa had other ideas for coping with the situation. She jumped in the lake two or three times a day.

"Do you do that to keep clean or just because you like to swim in the nude?"

She just beamed happily.

Unfortunately for his concentration, she always swam in the nude. Whenever he saw her moving towards the lake, he could no more stay peeling logs than he could stay still and let the flies get him. The sight of her naked body aroused him tremendously. He had never really grown accustomed to her. She always excited him. For him, her attraction had never diminished. He never failed to jump in after her. And thus it was that so much of the time, of so many of their days, was spent making love.

Whenever he thought about what was going to happen to her, he thought about these times — when she lived things totally, when she was so excited about everything — and when she was so exciting. He saw too well what would be gone.

Shane's work time was spent with the long, straight, spruce trees that would form the walls of their cabin. He cleared their cabin site of them and kept the ones that were straight. He set aside the other ones to use later for an outbuilding.

Theresa planted potatoes, lettuce, carrots, broccoli, onions, and other vegetables to provide them with a variety of fresh vegetables for a year. After she finished with the garden, she worked with Shane on the logs. She helped take the branches off with the axe. They both struggled to strip the bark from the trees, although it was less of a struggle in the late spring, when the sap was running, than it would have been in the fall.

The most laborious of the tasks was the stripping of the bark. It was harder and longer than cutting the trees and took many days. To do it, they used the drawknife, one of the tools they had made.

Mostly, they took time off from work — to dream, as Patrick Matchewan would have said. In mid-day when it was hot or when the flies were worst, they took off in the canoe for a trip around the little island lake. On the very hot still days the water was like glass. The brilliant disk of the sun shone on them from below as well as from above. They always hugged the shore of the lake, never crossing it directly. "That's the Indian way," Shane said. First, they wanted to see what was on the shore. They could glide along in the canoe five feet from the shore — out of reach of most of the flies — and look for edible plants and tea. As well, he looked intently for animal tracks. Shane tried to pinpoint good spruce and cedar, which he could later use to make a birch-bark canoe, a "real" canoe, as he said.

II

What they liked most in those early summer days while they were setting up their camp was to make a fire outside in the evening and then cook over the fire. After the meal was over, they'd sit by the fire in each other's arms and look into it. The warmth of the fire was soporific, and many times they woke up in the middle of the night to a cold fire after having fallen asleep.

They worked in short but steady stints on the cabin. When they at least had cut enough wood, the fly season was well on the wane. They laid four large logs on the ground for a base and put the first two wall logs on top. They made notches by chopping through the half-log and forming a cup for the log below. It was as tedious and long as stripping the bark.

After their log cabin was finished, Shane and Theresa made their first trip to Casey. It was ostensibly a supply trip but they also made it an occasion for a celebration of the completion of their cabin.

There were only a few families in the village. They spent a little time in the village's only bar, telling those who asked something about where they lived and what they were doing. They met an older couple who put them up for the night and helped them locate some plywood and shingles to take back to the cabin the next day. The older couple proved to be a godsend to Shane and Theresa. After Shane had inquired about where they could buy a larger wood stove than the very small one they had brought with them, the couple offered to look for one and for other things they might need. They would look around the village and, if they found anything, they would store it at their place. Shane and Theresa could then come look and buy the items or return them if they had no use for them. It was in this way that Theresa acquired the large bed she wanted. "I'm going to make a nice log cabin quilt for it," she smiled excitedly.

Back on the train that first morning after returning from Casey, they got off at their stop and left most of the materials again in the woods, taking only one sheet of plywood and some shingles.

By the end of July, the cabin was completed and the wood stove was moved in.

They furnished most of the cabin with furniture that they made from logs. What they lacked they were able to buy from people in Casey.

The front door of the cabin — and the two windows on that side — faced the cove and the small island offshore and to the left. It faced north and, on a few nights, gave them a chance to look at the aurora borealis with only the window open. The stove sat against the west wall of the cabin; in a corner on the east side was their bed and just across from that, under a front window, was a dry sink and a counter. They took their water from the lake and constructed an outdoor toilet in the trees in back of the cabin.

Chapter Twenty-One

I

Despite all the hard work, Theresa didn't complain. Shane couldn't see any real physical change in her, except that she got short of breath more easily and had lost a few pounds. He attributed the weight loss to the exercise because he himself had lost weight. She was taking medication and they both knew that the medication prevented the leukemia from spreading. Shane thought that the pregnancy helped Theresa maintain her appetite.

Shane watched Theresa often as she worked, dreading what it would be like without her. Without the noise and pollution of the city they had settled into a truly rich existence, with the barest of essentials, able to relate only to each other. Even in the city when things had gone well, they had not gone this well; here the earth and sky were part of their being together, the water was good, and the air was redolent with spruce and pine. Theresa took the trillium — the lilies of the wild — that bloomed around the cabin and kept them fresh in a vase on their dinner table. They ate wild onion, cattail shoots, and skunk cabbage in salads and round patches of wild strawberries and raspberries. Lac des Îles had rarely been fished. The little lake supplied them with abundant catches of northern pike. Shane and Theresa filleted them and then grilled them on a fire in front of the cabin.

One night they sat near the fire. There was a display of northern lights in the north. The Indian name for this phenomenon — *wawati* — was Theresa's family name.

"Do you think it's the sunlight reflecting from the glaciers at the North Pole?" Shane asked.

"I don't know," Theresa said, as she cuddled in his arms. "The old people say that the rainbow is really the spirits of dead wildflowers."

Shane still couldn't tell how Theresa was reacting to her illness. She seemed to be taking it quietly. She never actually mentioned it.

The black-fly season was over by the end of July, as was the hardest part of their work on the cabin. All that remained on the interior was a small amount of finishing work and the making of the furniture. Plants of the forest would continue to provide them with much of their food until the garden was ready for harvesting.

Wild plants also provided them with some of their most harrowing moments — thanks to Theresa's need to find out empirically what was good and what wasn't. While Shane put the finishing touches on the cabin, Theresa busied herself looking through a book they had on Indian uses of wild plants.

"Too bad that knowledge was taken away from you when you were growing up," Shane said.

When Theresa felt she had a clear understanding of a plant, she went out to locate it. Often after searching an entire afternoon, she would decide that they probably were a little too far north for the plant to survive.

She tried making many teas from common trees and smaller plants. And she discovered many of the plants she was looking for that she hadn't previously found. Invariably, at supper, she'd create some new concoction for them to try.

Theresa felt that plant discovery was her area and that therefore it was her responsibility to try out what she found before serving it to Shane.

"You're too beautiful to go on serving as a guinea pig," Shane said. "Be careful."

But often he caught her with a grimace of distaste on her face while she was puttering around sampling something. Twice he found her vomiting something up.

Shane showed her once a plant he knew — Labrador tea. Patrick Matchewan had shown it to him, had told him only its Indian name, and Shane had quickly forgotten it. It had a slender, shiny leaf with a furry underside. "This is a fine tea," he said. "Patrick made it for us often at night. It puts you to sleep."

"Let's pick some then," Theresa said.

"Yes, but Patrick said that you have to be careful. He said that there is a plant exactly like this but with a shiny underside to the leaf that is extremely dangerous. He took me to one and showed me what it looked like."

They gathered enough Labrador tea that day to last them for a while. And often they brewed it by their outside fire before going to bed in the evening.

"This is good tea," Theresa said. "Did the Indians drink it often?"

"I don't know."

"If they did, it's no wonder they slept so well."

One day not long after, Shane was working in back of the cabin. Theresa was going back and forth to the woods as she usually did, carrying plants in her hands on the return trip.

Something worried Shane after one of her trips. He saw smoke coming from the chimney, and he assumed she was brewing one of her teas. Invariably she brought out a cup for him, both as a refreshment and, he knew, to see his satisfaction at her having found a new herb.

This time his worry grew because he did not see her for some time after she had started her fire. He called to her, but there was no answer. He rose to go to the cabin, called again, and got no answer.

When he entered the door of the cabin, he saw her sprawled on the floor. "Theresa!" he exclaimed. He knelt down and shook her roughly. She came to — partially. "What is it! What is it!" he shouted.

"Labrador tea," she could barely mutter.

He swore. And he knew very well it was not Labrador tea but the other plant. He rushed to their little shelf that held jars containing various dried plants they had collected. There was one Patrick had shown him, an emetic. He took the jar from the shelf, grabbed a mug, and put some of the dried leaves in, pulverising them as much as he could with his fingers. She had left the tea kettle on the stove and he poured the still-hot water into the mug, trying to hurry the brewing.

He knelt down again, cradling her head in his left arm.

"Try to sip the tea," he said.

He held the mug to her lips until, after a long while, she had drunk most of it. Then he picked her up and laid her in bed. Nervously he attended her, waiting to see if the tea would have an effect. Patrick Matchewan hadn't made it clear what the plant resembling Labrador tea would do, only that its effect was no good. Shane knew that it must come up. He watched her. She seemed to be sleeping peacefully, until finally she moaned and started writhing. Concerned, he leaned forward — just as she turned to him and vomited. She vomited heavily. As uncomfortable as he was, Shane felt relieved.

He cleaned her up — and himself — and after she slept it off, her malaise had passed.

II

Catches of northern pike from the lake and trout from surrounding streams were a large supplement to their diet. When they needed supplies, Shane and Theresa hiked the four miles south to the Canadian National tracks, flagged down the late afternoon train going east and spent a night or two in Casey.

Theresa worked on her log-cabin quilt. "I want to finish it for the cold weather," she explained to Shane.

Often, as they went to bed at night in the big bed with the fluffy pillows, Shane read to Theresa from a book as she fell asleep. They talked of the peace they never had in the city, of being truly alive, as people seldom were.

"I know the secret of the woods," Theresa announced one day.

"The secret of the woods? I didn't know there was one."

"The secret of the woods is that the more you come in contact with the wild, the more you're drawn into it. It's sort of like seduction. For every motor and device of civilization you leave behind, you become more a part of this and you're drawn in even further. It's good when you see how easy it is to live in the bush, and how much you grow to need this kind of life."

III

One mid-July afternoon they left their work to go canoeing around Lac des Îles, as they often did when they wanted to be in the canoe but did not want to take an overland trip to another lake.

"You won't let me paddle," Shane complained.

Theresa smiled and went on paddling from the stern. She enjoyed paddling her canoe and her man around the lake.

At the end of the afternoon it started to rain, and as Shane was without a paddle, Theresa paddled briskly to get them back to the cabin — but not before they got soaked. Although it wasn't cold and there was only a slight rain at the time, they were chilled in their sodden clothes. They beached the canoe and hurried into the cabin.

"Let's get into some dry clothes and I'll make a fire to get the chill out," Theresa said.

"I've got another idea," Shane responded.

"There is no other idea. I'm shivering."

"Not what you think. I'm thinking of something Patrick said."

"What was that?"

"I think Patrick believed in rain."

"So do I. That's the best thing for the garden."

"No. I mean for people," Shane said. "He thought it was good for people. He said that only the white man didn't like rain; he had to hurry out of it. He had to avoid getting wet. He told me that in the old days Indians no more minded being rained upon than they minded that the sun should shine on their faces or that the wind should blow through their hair. They appreciated all the elements, and they liked being touched by them."

He reached over to Theresa's hand to stop her from pulling a dry pair of pants from the chest of drawers.

"I'm freezing," she said, and her body shook.

He gently had her put the pants back and lead her by the hand out of the cabin.

"Let's see what it's like," he said.

They wore no clothes or shoes. Theresa was still shivering so Shane put his arm around her. The steady rain continued. Shane admitted to himself that he was quite cold — but he dare not for the moment admit it to her.

Then a strange thing happened. The rain had by then completely drenched them. Their hair was soaked. It was raining so hard that the rain washed the mud from their feet as they walked. Shane was relaxed and, to his own surprise, he no longer felt cold.

"The rain is warm. It feels good," he said.

But under his arm, Theresa was still shivering, her face turned down toward the ground as if not to think about the cold rain. He expected her to bolt for the cabin at any minute.

He took his arm away from her. "Relax," he said, "The rain isn't cold." She shivered. "Feel it. You'll be surprised."

They walked on a little through the woods. Theresa looked very dubious but she tried to relax. She took a deep breath.

She seemed to be more at ease. She stopped shivering. She walked on easily. She liked to go barefoot whenever she could, but she never before had gone barefoot and nude in the rain. Shane could see that she was beginning to enjoy it.

In a moment, a faint smile came to her face. "I'm sorry, Shane," she said.

They walked in the woods around the cabin. Theresa absolutely revelled in the rain.

"Were we ever cold!" she laughed.

"It must have had something to do with being soaked in clothes."

"Maybe it was the way we were thinking too."

Whatever it was, Theresa felt an unbridled joy. Seeing her like this always brought joy to Shane in turn. And inevitably — more often now — he thought about what was going to happen to her. It increased his determination to seize every moment of togetherness out of the time they had left.

They held hands and walked slowly through the trees, stepping over some of the deadfalls in the understory. Shane stopped and leaned over to kiss Theresa on the shoulder. Their bodies were warm and glistening in the rain. Shane ran his hand over Theresa's back. He loved the feel of her in the warm rain.

He stopped and drew her to him. Her body was wet and warm against his. He had never felt closer to her physically than he did now. He held her tightly because he wanted to remember forever how her body felt at this moment. He kissed her on the front and side of her neck and finally on the mouth. He kissed her long and intensely in a way that somehow transcended passion. They kissed not only for that moment but also for years to come.

Theresa was caught up in their passion. When they had kissed for a long while, and were still holding each other in the rain, Shane reached with his right leg to her inner left leg and gently moved it to the side. Then he got down on his knees before her, held her to him and kissed her long and dearly.

Chapter Twenty-Two

I

After mid-summer, Theresa's health began to deteriorate. The deep tan she had acquired at the beginning of summer began to fade. She became shorter of breath. Her weight loss, while not great, was noticeable. Her appetite was good, but Shane attributed that solely to stimulants and dared not stop them. Also, she was capable of doing less work. It was as if her internal clock was telling her to slow down.

There was a surplus of berries that summer. In rapid succession they ate strawberries, Juneberries, wild cherries and raspberries, then blueberries.

In the second week of August, the blueberries ripened and covered the ground like a carpet of blue and green. Some of the berries were as big in diameter as a thumbnail, and so heavy they pulled down the branches until they touched the ground. They picked and dried blueberries to last for many months. They ate the berries off the bush, dried them, canned jams, cooked puddings, and baked pies.

Although Lac des Îles was home to many birds, none was as gregarious as the whiskey-jack. Aware of when the smallest crumb of food left the cabin, they came crying down for it, one or two at a time. At first, Theresa threw them bits of food. Then she noticed how near to her they seemed willing to come to get a treat. She dropped the food closer and closer to her body. In a few days, one ventured to take food from her hand.

"Somehow, the animals always seem to warm up to you much sooner than they do to me," Shane said.

A short while after that, noticing their boldness, she put a square of bread in her mouth and tipped her head back. She heard the bird make an inquisitive pass. Then he flew, pulled up and perched on her chin, neatly picking the bread from her mouth. Eventually, they learned to pick the bread from between her fingers on the fly.

One night they again made their fire outside the cabin. Theresa brewed some Labrador tea. She was full of news of her day, taming the whiskey-jacks.

"I bet I could tame this whole bush with enough time," she said, not aware of all the implications in her statement.

"I bet you could," said Shane.

Theresa had made friends with one little whiskey-jack. "He's a profiteer but he is a charmer all the same. He'll make friends with anyone if there's a piece of bread in it for him."

"Patrick said that a man should pick an animal he likes and study its Indian ways. He said that you could learn to understand where it lives, how it moves and the sounds it makes. He said that animals really want to talk with man."

"I wonder," Theresa said. "I was thinking that about the whiskey-jack. Maybe he'd make special sounds when he wanted certain things. I tried to distinguish his different sounds but I didn't have any luck. I couldn't learn another language at university. How am I going to learn whiskey-jack?"

"I think you could. I saw Patrick say some things to wild animals, and they responded. I swear they did. It was one of the strangest things I've ever seen."

"Are you sure he could talk to them?" Theresa said.

"Patrick could communicate with them. He could get a beaver to swim close to his canoe. All the whiskey-jacks were his friends, of course. And if he met a fox in the woods, he'd mumble something, and the fox would not bolt. When I asked him how he did it, he agreed that he could communicate with animals more than his children could communicate with them, but he also said that he was unable to talk with the animals as well as his father and people of earlier generations. He thought that if you looked at it that way, going back through the generations, there must have been a time when the Indians could talk directly to the animals."

Encouraged by her success with the whiskey-jack, Theresa started to work on a nearby beaver family. She first found the underwater entrance to the lodge and placed food — poplar branches — on the ground a few feet from it. Then she went home. She repeated this several times, always at the same hour of the day. The beaver always took the food. After having made them used to receiving the food at the same time every day, she stayed within sight when she delivered it to the spot. Then she moved closer. And every time she moved closer, she allowed a few days at each distance. In two months, the beaver were eating from her hand.

II

In early August, Shane and Theresa had begun building a birch-bark canoe. They found a large stand of birch trees on the north shore of Lac des Îles.

"Poor Patrick," Shane said, "I feel guilty. He has to hire someone with a pick-up truck and go miles to get bark for a canoe, and we find it right at our front door."

Much of the area hadn't been logged so it was with minimum searching that they found an ideal large birch. They made a ladder of hardwood poles. Shane used it to climb the trunk. With an axe, he made a cut sixteen feet down the trunk, and then they carefully removed the large sheet of bark.

Back in front of the cabin, they prepared spruce root. The roots were taken from beneath spruce trees and split evenly along the length of the root before the thin bark of the root was peeled off. The roots were then rolled in a coil and kept in water until used.

"The flies seem to like the spruce root," Theresa said, smiling and happy, in a way, in her predicament. She rose to make a smudge. She was happy when they were working together.

Shane looked at her. At times she looked somewhat pale; other times her colour was deep and vibrant. It did appear that she had lost a little weight. But he probably had as well; the activity was good for them both.

"I think we can probably count on the flies helping us at every stage of the canoe-building process," Shane said.

Strips of cedar served as the gunwales. They felled a tall, straight cedar tree and began by splitting the log in half, lengthwise. Then the two halves were split and the quarters split again. From there, they split off cedar strips. The five thwarts, made of birch, braced the gunwales apart, were fitted into them in mortises and anchored there by wooden pegs driven down through the gunwale and thwart — and, later, by the spruce-root lashing. The outside of the bark was the inside of the canoe. With two cedar pieces for each gunwale, the bark was sandwiched between, trimmed and lashed with spruce root. "This is the best part!" said Theresa enthusiastically. "I like the sewing with the spruce root."

The two stems were formed by splitting two cedar battens, immersing them in water for a few days and then bending them to the bow profile. Shane put them in place in the bow of the canoe, trimmed the bark to fit, and then lashed them in with spruce root.

"Ooof!" said Theresa on one of their building days, when it was especially hot and the flies had come up. She wiped the sweat from her brow and took a swipe at the flies, all the time trying to lash the gunwale with spruce root.

"Boy, is this a long job," she said.

"It takes a long time. Taking time is the Indian way."

To provide the framework of the canoe, they made ribs from cedar battens. They soaked these in water for a few days and then poured boiling water over them and bent them, forming them to the hull shape of the canoe.

A day-long trip through the woods from spruce tree to spruce tree got them the gum they needed to seal the canoe's seams. They looked for scars in the spruce and usually found gum deposits flowing from them. Back in front of the cabin, they boiled the gum and added animal grease to keep the gum from cracking. They applied the gum to the seams of the canoe with a small spatula. The gum dried in seconds. After having tested the canoe in the water, Shane carved out paddles from two lengths of ash. The birch-bark canoe looked fine; it was sturdy and — at forty pounds — weighed less than their commercially-made canoe.

"Well, what do you think of it?" Shane asked.

"*Kitci kwenatciwan*," she said approvingly. It is beautiful. They were out on their maiden voyage in the birch-bark canoe. It was gliding through the water quietly, with Theresa paddling in the bow and Shane in the stern.

"It floats easily. It's really light."

"If you take it by yourself, you'll have to make sure your weight keeps it in the water or the wind will get you. You'll have to put a big rock in the bow."

Thereafter Theresa took the canoe out often alone. She usually asked Shane to come with her in the other canoe, but there was something about the bark canoe that made her want to experience it alone. Her favourite trip was to comb the shore of the lake looking for Labrador tea and other herbs she could use. She soon cut out portages with an axe to the other lakes close by, made trips by herself for the day, and once overnight. She had quickly learned how to lift the birchbark canoe onto her shoulders and soon profited from the knowledge by carrying it often. Despite her gradually weakening condition, she often carried the canoe up to the cabin rather than leaving it down by the lake.

"We did a good job," Shane said, as Theresa set the canoe down after carrying it up from the lake one afternoon. He ran his hand along the goes sealed with spruce gum and the gunwales lashed with spruce root. He had tea ready for her.

"I've missed a lot over the years," she said.

"*Mitanawe*," he agreed, with some sadness.

Then he thought it better to change the subject.

"The bark canoe is pretty trusty."

"You can say that again," she agreed. "You can smash it like crazy in a rapid, and it won't puncture."

"May I ask how you know that?" He eyed her suspiciously.

She demurred.

"All right, where did you go?" he demanded.

"On that little quarter-mile rapid between Lac Écarté and Lac à la Truite. I wanted to see how the canoe would hold up. And besides, it was fun. I went through five or six times."

"You might have upset. Those aren't easy rapids. And it doesn't take much to get in trouble."

Theresa only showed enough contrition as she thought was needed to let the issue pass.

They sat around for a while, both continuing to examine the canoe.

"It's a thing of beauty, isn't it?" Theresa marvelled.

Shane nodded. "I'm surprised we did so well. Patrick's lessons were well learned."

"You should consider it a gift to be skilled enough to make one," she said.

"Flattery will get you nowhere."

"Do you know that I almost revere this canoe? It's that beautiful."

"I'm glad somebody does. I'll tell you something I saw once that made me very sad. The only birch-bark canoe that I have seen was in Montreal. I was visiting a friend, and he told me one day that he had seen a birch-bark canoe at his neighbor's house. We went over and looked at it. It was a canoe that had once been pretty good. It was full size and well made. It may even have been made by Patrick Matchewan many years before. I don't know; I didn't know birch-bark canoes at the time. It was set up on carpenter's horses, had been filled with dirt, and was being used as a flower planter. Would you believe that it choked me up when I saw that? It was the only birch-bark canoe I had ever seen. And look what happened to it."

Theresa spent a great deal of time in the bark canoe now. Shane spent much time in the back of the cabin with the bucksaw, cutting wood for the winter.

A few days after Shane had told her about the other bark canoe he had seen, he returned from a long day at the wood-pile to find her puttering around in front of their cabin. With a load of dirt she had scrounged from the woods, along with some transplanted trillium and wood blocks for support, she had made a very attractive planter from their four-hundred-dollar, factory-made canoe.

"You're priceless," Shane said.

III

At the end of the summer, they harvested potatoes, onions, and the rest of the vegetables from the garden, as each ripened in turn.

Their summer in the wilderness drew to a close with the multi-coloured pastiche of the leaved trees which were here and there among the conifers that surrounded Lac des Îles. Days grew shorter and evenings got cold enough to put wood in the stove. Winter was not far away.

When Shane had put up most of the wood, he worked on things to amuse himself.

"Do you like mushy things?" he asked her one day.

"Depends."

He handed her a square piece of birch-bark that he had framed in cedar. He had burned a poem into it with the burning point of a stick.

"I wanted you to have this. It's Nootka," he said.

Theresa took it from him and read:

No matter how hard I try
to forget you

you always
come back to my mind
and when you hear me singing
you may know
I am weeping for you.

Chapter Twenty-Three

I

Winter announced its coming quietly, at first, with a few snow flurries at the end of September and more through the beginning of October. On the smaller lakes, including Lac des Îles, the lee began to creep out from the shore.

October was not a happy month for them, because it was cloudy most of the time. The overcast days had failed to set off the brilliant leaves that remained on the trees in the first part of the month. Their wood was put up, chores were minimal, and the most they could hope for in terms of diversion was to remain in the cabin and read, or make moccasins and snowshoes. Theresa's spirits sagged with the weather.

"I feel nauseous," she said one day.

"Your pregnancy is advancing," Shane pointed out. He liked the looks of her stomach rounding out. The pregnancy seemed to be putting some weight on her. "It's probably that."

"Or my sickness."

It was unlike her to complain about being ill.

Then, on the first of November, a foot of snow covered everything. Whipped by winds, the snow piled in drifts that nearly reached the gables of the cabin. Shane had made the mistake of building the door so that it opened out instead of opening in. Now the snow piled deep against the door; it couldn't be opened. He opened a window, climbed out into the snow and shovelled out the front door. That day he changed the door so they wouldn't be trapped again.

Theresa was bubbling with the excitement at the first big snowfall of the year. As soon as he had them dug out, they went off on snowshoes. She wouldn't have stayed in the cabin for anything. A foot of snow by itself would not have justified their using snowshoes, but drifts were so frequent that they could not have travelled any great distance without them, and Theresa was anxious to put them on for the first time of the season. Her strength was not sufficient for a long walk. Were it not for her excitement by the first snowfall, Shane doubted that she could have mustered the courage to walk outside the cabin. She was late in her pregnancy but had not gained appreciable weight. He knew that her pregnancy had nothing to do with her weakened state.

Shane could no longer mistake the changes that were coming over Theresa. It was as if the medicine no longer had any effect. She still took the palliatives daily but she was becoming gaunt and pale. She walked with more difficulty and did not go outside often. For the first time since he knew her, Shane saw Theresa as he had never seen her — pale, weak, and almost spiritless. She no longer had something to say every time he spoke to her. She didn't laugh as easily — she of the smile and laugh that struck people so strongly that it was the first thing they remembered about her. Sometimes, now, she only nodded her head at something she thought was funny. The painkillers were no longer masking her pain all the time, yet she barely showed it. She didn't want him to know. One time she went to the cabin door with him as he was leaving. She smiled at him as he turned to go and then, having forgotten something, he turned back, already a grimace of pain had returned to her face. She had tried to hide it but had not been able to. She knew it wouldn't be long now; they both knew it.

"You should go out more often," Theresa said. "You don't have to stay in the cabin because of me." She was sitting in a little rocking chair and working on a pair of moccasins.

"To be very truthful," he said, "I really don't enjoy going out of the cabin without you."

She squeezed his hand.

"And I hate to see you in here, only able to make it from the bed to the rocking chair." It was as close as he had ever come to pity.

"I miss not being able to fix meals," she said.

Shane did not know what to say to that. He studied her when she was not watching him. She was noticeably wan.

"I wonder if I should have insisted to the doctor that we come in the bush. You would have been more comfortable in Montreal," he said.

He was upset at himself the moment the words were out of his mouth; he could well see himself sliding into lugubriousness — the only thing they did not need at the moment.

"We did the right thing when we came here," Theresa said. Even her voice did not have the vitality it always had.

"I thought the cold would be fun," he said, "but that's not what you need."

She looked at him, apparently too tired to answer, and with a look that suggested she hoped he would discontinue such talk.

"Would you mind if I went off by myself for two or three days?"

Theresa was lying on top of the bedclothes as she often did now, propped up against a pillow and reading a book. She always gave the impression of enjoying long periods of reading, but Shane knew that it was only a kind of waiting.

She gave a big sigh of relief and smiled thankfully.

"So you feel it too," Shane said.

"I'm afraid so," she admitted. "We're becoming bushwhacky sitting here all the time with nothing to do but think. I thought of suggesting you go into Casey for a few days, but I didn't know how you'd take it. We need a little relief."

"Would you be alright?"

"Of course. I'll help you get your things ready."

But he was more concerned that she be well. He tried to think of everything. If she were well, she would have no trouble going outside to the woodpile. But not to take any chances, he piled five days' supply of wood and kindling inside the cabin a few feet from the stove. He placed matches at several places in the cabin so she couldn't lose them. He checked all the food to make sure there was enough. He brought in three large pails of drinking water from the lake so she would have enough in case of emergency. "And here's the potty pail," he said, placing another pail not far from the bed.

He put extra books by the side of the bed for her. And he put two more blankets on the bed in case she was not, for any reason, able to make a fire.

The rest of the day Shane spent preparing his own things to leave, the following morning. Theresa was right behind him with questions.

"Have you got enough food?" she asked, and Shane laughed that she was showing the same close attention to his welfare that he had shown to hers.

"I'm taking just barely enough for three days. I don't want to be weighted down."

"What happens if you break a leg and have to stay out longer?"

"That's not likely. It's more likely that I get homesick or cold after one night on the trail and decide to come back after two days."

"Remember what Patrick said about being careful."

II

Next morning he had his axe, snowshoes, and other gear ready at the door. Theresa had awakened early to make him breakfast. A topographical map was spread out on the table.

"I think I'll head up to Pointe à l'Indienne on Lac Kinonje, then circle around to this little lake here and back home." He pointed to a small lake three or four miles from the larger Lac Kinonje. "That's fifty miles round trip, maybe less."

"Isn't that a little far for three days?"

"If it is, I'll know by tomorrow morning and head back."

He kissed her and went outside to put his snowshoes on in front of the cabin. Theresa was shivering at the door of the cabin, shouting after him, "Be careful!"

He felt as though he had flown to Lac Kinonje. It was twenty miles but easy going once he had spotted a game trail that followed a large river. He walked easily along the trail. The snowshoes on the deep snow kept him well above the underbrush, brush that he would have to trudge through at any other time of the year. It felt good to be out in the woods.

In between brisk stints walking on the trail, he stopped to eat a little and to drink from the occasional hole through the ice of a fast-running stream. The water was so cold that he could only sip it. At noon he made a fire.

At four o'clock in the afternoon, much to his surprise, Shane came to the very broad Lac Kinonje. He made his fireplace against the flat side of a high rock so that heat would be reflected. It was already starting to become dusk. He had hoped to make his little three-day jaunt a bit of a challenge, but so far it had been easy, and he was a little disappointed. Not that he wanted to make trouble.

That night he laid his sleeping bag on spruce boughs near a fire and kept the fire going by feeding long dead-spruce poles into it at two-hour intervals, waking through the night to do so.

The next morning, he made a breakfast of side pork and some bannock that Theresa had made for him. A chipmunk and two chickadees came around to see if he would share. He threw some bannock crumbs on the snow for the chickadees. They cried, "Chick-a-dee-dee-dee! Chick-a-dee-dee-dee!" in excitement. To the chipmunk, he tossed little bits of fat from the side pork. The chipmunk gave feverish little smacking sounds as if to say, "What good friends we could become!"

After breakfast, he pointed toward the small lake three miles distant, which was his turnaround to go south again. He thought that if he had felt like going fast, he could easily have made it back to Theresa that day. He thought about her all the time. He'd spend some time camped at the lake and make an easy, fifteen-mile trek home tomorrow.

He had to go cross-country to the little lake, so for the first time on his trip he took his topographical map and compass out and held them in his hand. The branches were thicker here than they had been for him before. He had to use his axe.

He went up and down hills and across small, frozen creeks trying to make a straight line between Pointe à l'Indienne and the small lake. It made him a little nervous. Thinking back, it was actually the first time he had gone cross-country, relying on his skills of navigation, such as they were, and eschewing logging roads and rivers as guiding points.

Shane thought he was nearing the small lake — it had only been three miles away — and was looking forward to making very early camp and exploring the lake a little when he came down from a hill and saw a very broad stream in the next valley.

The creek was frozen over, but he knew by its width that it was probably fairly deep and would not have frozen solid — certainly not this early in the season. He viewed the crossing with trepidation. As a boy he had crossed frozen lakes and streams without hesitation. But the old people had made him very wary of walking on ice. Don't trust lake ice when there is heavy snow on it, they said. The snow covering may have kept it from freezing solid. One had to be very careful of river ice, they said.

A glance in both directions along the bank told Shane he'd be unlikely to find a better crossing elsewhere on the broad stream. He cut a twelve-foot maple pole to use in case he fell through the ice. And he did something the old people had always told him to do: he loosened the bindings of his snowshoes. If a man ever accidentally passed through the ice, the worst thing he could have on his feet was snowshoes, they said, because there was no way he could rise out of the water with them on.

Shane tucked his axe tightly in his pack. He loosened the snowshoe bindings and grabbed the maple pole in his right hand.

He walked slowly out on the ice, the other bank fixed in his attention. Slightly comforting was the fact that the snowshoes would distribute his weight over the ice in the same way they had over the powdery snow.

With small steps, sliding and not lifting the snowshoes, he edged away from the near bank. He heard the water flowing swiftly past under the ice, but it gave no clue as to the ice's thickness.

He slowed his already slow pace. The ice cracked. He stopped. He looked a little to the left and a little to the right, hoping that off to one side or the other the ice might be thicker. He inched slowly away from the spot and the ice cracked again. He tried to move his snowshoes a little backward and the ice cracked again. He would not be able to retreat. He held his breath. There was no way of telling the thickness or strength of the ice through the snow cover.

He took two small, sliding steps. There was no noise. Then, with a sharp crack and great splash, the ice gave way. His first thought was not his situation but Theresa's. The instant horror of the predicament was reduced to one thought: Would he see her again?

As Shane was pitched down into the cold, swiftly running water, his pack with its tumpline slipped from his forehead and fell into the water. Reacting to the surprise, he dropped the map and compass from his left hand and the maple pole from his right hand. Of all these, he retrieved the pole first, grabbing it tightly again before it hit the water.

Although the water was moving swiftly, it did not draw Shane downstream because his falling through the ice had left a hole; the maple pole bridged the hole, and he held on to it for his life. His pack, still floating, was an arm's length away, bucking against the ice. Shane grabbed the tumpline and put it again around his forehead. The map and compass were lost. Not yet experiencing the full chill of the water, he pulled mightily on the pole. He couldn't lift himself six inches. At first, he thought of removing the awkward pack from his forehead and back. But then he realized that it was not the real problem. The snowshoes were a powerful drag on his legs. He knew he'd die of exposure minutes after the cold water penetrated his clothing. He tried again, desperately, to lift himself, and even with all the strength he could muster, he was able to lift himself only a foot.

He remembered that he had loosened the snowshoe bindings and began to shake them off. Then he stopped. He might lose them. But the alternative was to lose his life. Then he thought that perhaps they'd float around in the hole in the ice as his pack had, and he'd be able to retrieve them. So he shook hard, first the right one and then the left, while holding tightly on to the pole with both hands. Both snowshoes came off with little trouble. But they both stayed under water long enough for the current to carry them under the ice.

Shane tried once again, and he felt much lighter. He boosted himself out of the water on to a ledge of thicker ice. With the pole still securely in hand and the pack flopping on his back, he did a spread-eagled crawl to the bank.

His only thought was to make a fire as quickly as possible. He stripped the lower dead branches of nearby spruce trees for kindling and pulled some loose bark from a birch. He took protected matches from his pack and in minutes had a fire going.

Over a big fire, he dried the wet clothes, huddling close to the fire as he waited. The chill he felt was from the close call he had and not from the cold. The fire felt good.

It was early afternoon, but he decided to make camp and examine the situation.

On the minus side, he had lost his snowshoes, map, and compass. Loss of the map and compass presented no problem; the next morning he'd simply backtrack to Lac Kinonje and then down to Lac des Îles along his snowshoe trail. Losing his snowshoes was something else again. He'd have to slow down to a crawl because the snow was deep in places, many places. The snowshoes would hardly have packed the trail down at all. And the extra effort he'd have to expend would cause trouble because he had little food left. The first day, he had eaten too much. The last day, he was hoping to eat a little in the morning and then to eat a meal in the evening with Theresa. Now he would certainly have to spend one extra night on the trail, and he'd have to budget his food drastically.

That night, in his camp by the fire, he was happy at the chance to rest up. Struggling through the snow without snowshoes was going to be hell, and he would need to be well rested.

It began to snow as he fell asleep. The wind came up. He was worried and couldn't sleep. If it should happen to snow ten or twelve inches, he'd lose the snowshoe trail.

Sometime late in the night, he awoke. The wind was still blowing but the snow was only coming down in light flakes. He reached for his pack, which had been sitting in the open, and felt it. Only a couple of inches of snow covered it. He went back to sleep, satisfied that his troubles appeared to be over.

Next morning he made a fire and had tea and bread. It was cloudy. He felt very well as he ate and looked across the stream at his snowshoe trail coming down to the ice. Snow had blown into the tracks but he could see where he had walked.

He crawled all the way across the ice this time and had no trouble. His problems started when he began walking in his old tracks. He sunk to his knees in the snow, slowing himself greatly. He stopped three or four times while walking to the top of the hill, and knew that he'd have to stop regularly all the way home.

When he reached the top of the small hill, he stopped to rest but then recoiled at what he saw before him. The two-inch powder, which had left the snowshoe tracks perfectly visible on the sheltered bank of the stream, had now been buffeted by the wind to fill in and smooth over completely his snowshoe trail of the previous day.

Shane's face was flushed. He took his pack down from his back and sat on it. He had no compass and no sun. With the sun out, he would have had no trouble heading in a generally southerly direction and reaching the CN tracks. His only hope was to keep on walking and try to find the snowshoe trail again.

He didn't want to imagine what would happen to Theresa if he couldn't make his way back to her.

He walked and rested and walked all day. Only once, right away, did he pick up the snowshoe trail again. But it disappeared after twenty yards. And still he had no sun, and no way to tell directions. The wind still carried the light snow around. Too late did he realize that he could have gone back to the little stream. Watercourses in his immediate area flowed roughly south and would all lead to the rail line. Now the lightly blowing snow would have covered up the tracks he made when he started out from the stream.

He had to keep on. Theresa needed him. Making camp a day or two to wait for clear weather was out of the question. He had almost no food left. He had to use his best judgment and give it a try.

He knew he was not making a half a mile an hour. The snow was deep and he had to try not to exert himself to avoid creating a sweat. Although he was warmly clothed, he knew that dampness could be the end of him.

As the day drew to a close, he continued to wander aimlessly. He would not be back with Theresa tonight, maybe not even tomorrow night. But she would begin to worry this evening and continue until she saw him again. He hoped she wouldn't remember how little food he had taken along. He hoped that her worrying would not cause her to try to come after him. That would be the worst thing she could do. He was comforted by the fact that she had confidence in him.

Shane made camp early. He knew he couldn't become any more lost in the dark than he could on a cloudy day, but he wanted to conserve his energy. The walking in the deep snow was costing him dearly. And now he had only bread left to eat. That, and some sugar to sweeten his tea. It seemed to him that he had enough sugar for several days, so he set about boiling a thick tea with spruce needles. Laced with sugar, it wasn't at all bad to drink. And high in Vitamin C, he thought, chuckling to himself. Mentally he made a short list of six or seven things he was likely to die of before he died of scurvy.

The next morning, he ate the last of the bread and drank some more spruce tea. If only the sun would come out, he thought, long enough for him to begin heading in a southerly direction. Even if it came out for only two hours. It would be long enough to make a straight line and make his fixes against distant trees — enough to hit the east-west train line eventually. But he saw no sun.

He remembered that the area around Lac Kinonje was of greater elevation than Lac des Îles and the Canadian National rail line. Even though he was going up and down hills constantly, he headed in a direction he thought was leading to a lower elevation.

He knew he was virtually out of food, but if he reached Lac des Îles this day — rather unlikely — or if he had to camp only once more, he'd be alright. But walking was much harder now. He counted one hundred steps, and after each set he stopped to rest. And his rest stops were growing longer.

The only comfort he had was that he thought he was going in a straight line and he seemed to be going to a lower elevation, although he wasn't sure.

At four o'clock in the afternoon, it was becoming dark. He wanted to travel a little further distance before setting up camp. Although he was tired as he never had been, and hungry as he never thought he could be, there was the flicker of encouragement left in him. He was sure that his guesswork navigation had cut at least a few miles from the thirteen or fourteen he thought had remained to him in the morning. A clear day tomorrow — or a lucky one — and he'd reach the tracks.

In the dusk ahead of him he saw a trail! Maybe a moose, he thought. And he'd certainly try to go after it, for he needed the meat. Or better yet, a trapper. Because of the new snow, the track had to be a fresh one. He was certain he could follow it in the dark, even by palpitation, and he might very well come upon the man's cabin — unless he had a snowmobile nearby that had sped him away. But even that would be good. A snowmobile trail would be much better to walk on than what he had.

When he reached the tracks in the snow, he saw that they were the ones he had made that morning.

Chapter Twenty-Four

I

If Shane ever had any doubt that he was in trouble, that doubt was dispelled. There was no sun the next day. Spruce tea was not nourishing, however healthy it might be. The only thing it did was comfort him.

When he had his pack made up, he didn't know which way to go. The circle route would be no good. But he had to move, so he began putting one foot in front of the other slowly. For the first time since he was a boy, he prayed. He prayed not to return to the cabin, but to see Theresa again — although he couldn't accomplish one without the other. He wanted to see her once more.

Several hours after he began his slow walk, he glimpsed the sun through a passage in the clouds. For the first time in days, he felt elated. He calculated that it was close to the meridian because it had been four or five hours since the sun rose. He headed off towards it, and his pace picked up.

Although the sun had disappeared almost as quickly as it had appeared, he now felt that he had a reasonably good fix on a southerly direction. After an hour, though, his pace again slowed, as much from lack of confidence in his direction as from overpowering fatigue.

Depression and fatigue grew as the day wore on. His one hope was that the sighting he had taken on the sun would help him find the rail line.

By mid-afternoon he knew he could walk no further. He made camp and brewed some tea for the hunger that was tearing at his stomach. But the tea didn't seem to help, and the hunger kept him from sleeping.

He was without energy, but he began all the same the next morning. He sighted back along his trail and then ahead in a line he hoped was heading in a generally southern direction.

All morning he struggled, by now only a few steps at a time. At noon, or what he thought to be noon, the sun once again was visible through the clouds. He corrected his direction, but only slightly. He thought that his bearings were good. He was going in the right direction. But his pace was slow. He thought he might be covering one mile, at most, in two hours. He knew he'd have to stop soon. If only he had food, he'd be safe. But there was no wire for a snare and no rabbit tracks. He could think of nothing else to eat from the bush surrounding him. Spruce tea was the only food he had. All the roots that the old people harvested were buried under snow until spring.

He made camp once again in the early afternoon, unable to go on. By now, he felt that the tea helped him to sleep. But it also made him wake up to urinate often.

In his nightmarish sleep he dreamed that he saw Theresa in the distance, but died of starvation before he could reach her. In the light of day, he knew that his nightmare wasn't far from the truth. Because of his exhaustion, he might not be able to make it there.

There was light the following day — sunlight. Brilliant sunlight and a bright blue sky. 'What a cruel joke!' he thought. There was no question that he was headed in the right direction and that the tracks of the railroad were probably no more than five or six miles distant. But he had no way to walk there, no energy.

He moved, nevertheless, telling himself that he now had the right direction and would never lose it. If he had to do one mile a day and build a fire four times a day, he would reach home. But as it approached noon, he began to see that even this seemed to be an impossibility. He had not made one half of a mile in the morning — and would not make another half mile in the afternoon. Whether he had been in an area where it had snowed more heavily or whether he was reaching the end of his strength, he did not know.

Then, as he came over a small rise, he saw tracks in the snow. He had run into his own trail again! He collapsed in the snow.

He regained consciousness later, how much later he didn't know. How could he possibly have rejoined his trail, he asked himself in utter hopelessness. He was sure that he had made a good sighting on the sun — and his trail had been as straight as he could make it. He lifted his head to look at the tracks that crossed twenty feet in front of him. They wandered back and forth in the shallow gully between two low elevations. And he saw how, with such erratic wandering during the day, he could easily have double-backed on himself. He pounded his fist in the snow and shook his head in frustration.

Then he raised his head again and froze looking at the tracks. They were not his tracks. He had stumbled and fallen many times during the day, but he had never meandered as these tracks did.

He crawled quickly to the tracks, leaving his pack behind. A moose had passed through, probably a small one. The tracks were fresh and looked like the creature that made them was having as much trouble in the snow as Shane. The snow was so deep that it was clear how the belly of the moose was dragging in the snow.

Retrieving his pack, he made off after the moose in its tracks. Walking was much easier but he felt unfathomably weak. He pulled his axe from the pack.

He fell often now, more out of fatigue than resistance from the snow. But he was encouraged by the freshness of the tracks. And it was plain that the moose was as tired as he was.

Then he saw it, in a shallow depression. It was this year's calf, maybe eight months old now. Its belly was dragging in the snow, as he had seen from its tracks.

The yearling moose was framed in the branches of a spruce tree which, being disturbed, had dropped loads of snow upon the animal. It was struggling to move. As Shane neared, it struggled to flee. As he came upon it from the side, he brought down the axe as hard as his waning strength would allow. The animal revolted furiously at the initial blow, but Shane called upon a superhuman will and struck and struck again until the top of the animal's head was a bloody pulp and there was no movement. Falling on the carcass, he passed out from exertion.

Coming to a few moments later, he knew he hadn't the strength to cut the meat and gather wood for a fire. He remembered something the old people used to relate about dying Indians who needed nourishment immediately. He unsheathed his hunting knife, felt the moose's neck for the still pulsing jugular and forced the knife straight in.

Blood spurted. His hand darted out to stop it. With his hand on the wound, he lowered himself from the animal's back into the snow. Positioning himself next to the neck, he removed his hand and quickly put his mouth over the wound. He drank eagerly.

There was a great amount of blood. It ran down his chin. But it was warm and life-giving. He thanked the moose for giving its life for him.

After having drunk briefly, he stopped up the wound with a handful of snow and put the pack against it. Then he reclined against the moose and slept.

For several hours, he drank the blood of the moose intermittently, until the flow stopped. Then, with slightly renewed strength, he built a fire and made camp for the night.

Later he cut meat from the haunch of the moose and roasted it. For once, he had nourishment with his spruce tea. He knew he was safe now. He ate as much meat that night as he thought he could safely handle. He roasted more the next morning for breakfast, and cooked all he could carry for the trail. A few days later, when he had regained his strength, he could come back for the rest of the meat.

Shane walked much more strongly that day, sure he was going in the right direction and confident that he had his strength back.

Late that afternoon, he was making his way up a hill and saw beyond the hill the telltale break in the trees that always indicated a river below. The break in the trees was even, and he suspected he had found his way.

When he was standing on the crest of the hill, he was looking down on the Canadian National tracks.

Chapter Twenty-Five

I

With the deeper cold of late November, it was becoming more and more difficult to find a wide range of activities with which to keep busy. Theresa had her moccasins. Shane brought wood in and a few times went ice fishing. Theresa liked the northern pike he prepared for them. He baked beans, he made pea soup, and he fetched potatoes and turnips from the little root cellar he had made beneath the cabin.

The wood stove heated the cabin well during the day. In late evening, Shane stoked the stove for the night but it did not keep the cabin warm until the next morning. Their bodies, together under the quilt — Shane's arm around Theresa — and the blankets kept them comfortable until dawn. And in the morning when the sun pushed away the cold night and the temperature was at its coldest, Shane jumped out of bed in his long underwear, threw his wool shirt and heavy pants on quickly, and lit the fire in the stove. When warmth began to filter through the cabin, he made breakfast for the two of them, with Theresa sometimes peeking over the top of the quilt and the warmth it provided.

One evening after he had read to her, he turned out the oil lamp and crawled into bed. Theresa was listless with fatigue and weakness, but still awake. He took her in his arms. "I love you," he said. And she gave a little nod of her head, unable to give any other response.

One day in early December, Theresa began having labour pains. The birth would be very premature. She hadn't been out of bed for many days, Shane gave her something the doctor had given him to induce delivery. In view of some of the troubles they already had had, the birth was almost an anticlimax. Theresa was taking medicine to relieve the pain from the leukemia, which was now permeating her body. With all the medication, the birth was hardly more than an additional, temporary pain. Shane thought that they were lucky to have such an easy delivery. The baby was healthy, and her mother survived the birth.

Theresa's eyes glowed when the baby was placed in her arms, though she was too tired to smile.

Some minutes later, Shane made a weak tea for Theresa and held it up to her lips. She took a sip.

"What will we call our daughter?" he asked.

Theresa closed her eyes and did not say anything. At last, Shane thought that she was not going to answer and was about to ask the question again.

Then Theresa was able to open her eyes. She said quietly, "Victoria."

Shane made a little hammock out of a rope and blanket. He hung it from the celling next to the bed. The baby was lulled to sleep by swinging the hammock back and forth. He tied a little strip of cloth on the hammock so that Theresa could pull it when she had the strength.

Once, when she had sufficient strength to speak, she said, "My mother used to rock us in a blanket like this when we were at Ottawa Lake." She said it in a tone that suggested that she was surprised that the memory had come back.

Suffering alternately through pain, medication and fatigue, Theresa's periods of alertness — and an occasional slight increase — were few. She managed to rise from the bed only once.

More often, she seemed to be suffering from a quiet kind of pain. Shane could tell when she had a little strength, for then she would hold Victoria close to her. At night, he could sometimes tell that the disease was tormenting her.

One night when she was suffering, he got out of bed, put his moccasins and toque on, and lit the oil lamp. He put the lamp on the table and gathered up all the medicines the doctors had given him. He placed them next to the lamp and looked them over. Theresa was moaning quietly at the pain she was experiencing.

The doctors had explained the effects of all the medicines to Shane. They had described the recommended doses at various stages of her illness. Shane had administered different doses of the several medicines over a period of time. The doctors told him that at some point — when the suffering became very intense — the dose needed to deal with all the pain might prove lethal.

Shane sat for a while and looked at the medicine bottles. Then he walked over without any medicine and sat on the bed and looked at her.

After a few moments, she awoke and looked up at him.

He looked at her with sorrow in his eyes. "I wish I could do something to relieve your pain," he said. "If only there was something I could do."

She didn't answer for a time. Then she said, "There is." It was hard for her to talk.

"What is it?"

"Speak to me in Indian."

Chapter Twenty-Six

I

Shane was no longer interested in making snowshoes. Hunting was not possible. The newly fallen snow had no animal tracks; in the first deep cold of the winter, the animals were hardly moving around. Even had they been, his enthusiasm was not there. Nor could he develop an interest in attempting to catch some northern pike through the ice.

It seemed to be getting dark in the middle of the afternoon now. Shane prepared supper for the three of them. After they — now meaning him and the baby — ate, he washed the dishes and tried to read for a while. When, inevitably, his concentration was not there, he went to bed.

One night when the oil lamp was out and they were in bed, she said to him, "You'll put trillium on the grave?"

Shane promised.

He went out just before Christmas and came back with a small spruce tree. Set in a corner of the cabin, it was the only note of lightness in an otherwise doleful time. He tried to sing Christmas songs to the baby, but with Theresa unable to participate, it was only a pathetic effort. He made for Victoria a little straw doll that she would be able to play with in a few months.

It snowed heavily the night of Christmas. Snow covered two windows and continued to fall all night. This was their warmest night. The snow left an absolute silence. Theresa whispered to him that it was just this kind of peace that they had sought when they came to Lac des Îles.

Just after Christmas, a bitter cold was visited upon Lac des Îles. Drinking water in the pail in the cabin was frozen solid in the mornings. Shane could not fold back the heavy quilt covering Theresa until he had lit the wood stove, and until he was sure that the cabin was quite warm. As soon as it was warm enough, he pulled back all the covers save one.

Theresa no longer seemed to hear or understand when Shane read to her in the evening before he came to bed. She was gone now, gone to any of the vital forces she had once known. Hers was a wasted body and no more.

As Shane finished reading one evening, she motioned for him to come near.

"Bring the baby to bed," she whispered.

Shane took Victoria from the hanging cradle and placed her between the two of them. He held them both close to him all night.

In the morning, Theresa was dead.

He buried her beneath a small stand of pine trees in back of the cabin. He worked all day with axe and shovel to get through the frozen ground. And all he thought about was how much life was gone from his life.

He planted trillium over the grave when the snow went. The lilies of the forest kept her and bobbed up and down in the breezes of spring.

MORE FROM BARAKA BOOKS

FICTION

Washika, A Novel
Robert A. Poirier

THE ADVENTURES OF RADISSON
1 Hell Never Burns
2 Back to the New World
3 The Incredible Escape
Martin Fournier

THE NICKEL RANGE TRILOGY
The Raids
The Insatiable Maw
Mick Lowe

NONFICTION

America's Gift
What the World Owes to the Americas
and Their First Inhabitants
Käthe Roth & Denis Vaugeois

Journey to the Heart of the First Peoples Collections
Musées de la civilisation
Marie-Paul Robitaille, Director

The Complete Muhammad Ali
Ishmael Reed

The Franz Boas Enigma
Inuit, Arctic and Science
Ludger Müller-Wille